The Impossible Murder of Headless in Houston

An Imogene Chaplin mystery

Hafeez Diwan

The Impossible Murder of Headless in Houston

Copyright © 2006 by Hafeez Diwan

This book is a work of fiction. Names, characters, places, and incidents are the product of the author's imagination or are used fictitiously. Any resemblance to actual persons, living or dead, business establishments, organizations, events, or locales is entirely coincidental.

PART ONE: BODY

1

George Zimaresh was found without his head in a locked room that no one could have left without leaving the door unlocked. I should add that his head was not found in the room with him. These were the plain facts, facts that I encountered one night shortly after I arrived in Houston. I know it seems confusing, maybe even impossible. In the end, of course, it all became so obvious, so straightforward, and not confusing or puzzling at all. But that was later, after the discovery of the head and all that followed. Am I making sense? Probably not. I always have this problem when I'm telling a story, even if it is absolutely true and happened to me, and I know it like the back of my hand. Very well, I shall take the advice of those who tell us to tell it like it is, starting at the beginning, going through the middle, and not stopping until the end.

* * *

In fact, I'll start a little before the beginning and put things in context for you.

My name is Imogene Chaplin. I am a pathologist. I used to be in Potokapaw, but you've probably never heard of it, right? Not many people have; even I wouldn't have heard of it had I not spent nearly all my life there.

I left Potokapaw for a very simple reason. Potokapaw is a beautiful, small, Southern university town in Alabama. After thirty-six years, however, I'd had enough of it. I sought a new scene. And that is how I came to be in Houston, which is not exactly beautiful, being rather flat and not very scenic. But Houston is a big city, millions of people, plenty of great restaurants, and there's a lot happening—too much, as I found out.

Finding a full-time job as a surgical pathologist in Houston was not that easy. Let me take a detour and explain something: Few people on the planet, I have noted, are fully aware of exactly what surgical pathologists do for a living. Most people seem to imagine that all they do is autopsies and crime scene investigations, but this is what *forensic* pathologists do.

The surgical pathologist does something else. If you go to a doctor, and the doctor does a biopsy, or removes your gallbladder, or appendix, or a bit of your brain, the tissue is then processed, embedded in paraffin wax, then cut into really thin, microscopic slices, put on glass slides, and stained using certain dyes. The surgical pathologist then examines the glass slides with the stained tissue under the microscope; he (or she) "reads" the slides and comes to a diagnosis. This is what surgical pathologists do—and this is what I wanted to be doing all the time but couldn't (and still can't) because the pathology market in Houston was saturated at the time. The best I was able to find was a part-time job with a private pathology group (two days a week), with the hope and promise of being full-time and a partner in the future (which would mean big, really big money).

This part-time business left me with the rest of my time and, naturally, the desire for more money. I agreed to pitch in as a part-time forensic pathologist, working with my classmate Alec Spence, who is with the Houston Medical Examiner's Office. This is how I came to muck about with blood and bodily fluids—and, of course, the late George Zimaresh, minus his head, in a locked room.

A word about George Zimaresh, if only for the sake of completeness. For who hasn't heard of Zimaresh? The famed mystery writer, playboy, man about town. Unfortunately dead now, but he had it going well when he was around. His life, while he had it, was laced with stories of Zimaresh on the yacht, Zimaresh in Monaco, Zimaresh with such-and-such hot model; sordid, juvenile stuff about excessive amounts of sex, money, good food, alcohol—and did I mention sex? There was a considerable emphasis during his time on earth on the (successful) pursuit of sex. Apparently, Zimaresh was (he once told a reporter in an interview) in some sort of competition with a famous late European mystery writer who may have made love to as many as ten thousand women. Unbelievable? Perhaps, but it got Zimaresh hopping like an unstoppable bunny rabbit in the carnal domain. From what I came to hear, Zimaresh was an ambitious man, a man like many other ambitious men, for whom having a whole lot of everything still falls short of having enough. Perhaps he was even discontented in the midst of plenty, like so many others before and after him.

2

The first few weeks were uneventful. It was a lot of the usual sort of thing: plenty of dead old people, tormented lovers gassing themselves to death, shootings, and natural deaths of young people in their forties who keeled over and died of coronary thrombosis—that is to say, heart attacks. Likely brought on by stress, too much pressure, too little time, not enough money, the same old story. It was sad at first, but within a few days, it became boring and began to seem more and more like a job—a job that I would gladly be rid of as soon as the full-time position opened up at Culpepper, Fenn, and Witherspoon, LLC, the private pathology group where I was working two days a week.

Roy Culpepper, my boss, was often in my office, usually saying nothing very meaningful or important, and he was given to smacking his lips excessively. I found this habit of his disconcerting. It made him look like a lecher. Was he a lecher? Was he secretly fantasizing about me? I know I am not ugly and could even be considered attractive from one or two angles, especially when I tie my hair and pull it back over my ears like I was doing those days. I've noticed that I get more compliments from males whenever my ears are exposed, and so I wondered if it was this that was bringing out the lip-smacker lurking inside Roy Culpepper. Little did I know where this would lead, but I will get to it in good time.

Now, let me come to the fateful day. That day was very boring, to begin with. Four natural deaths—all fairly old people—got the day started. In the afternoon, I had a brief interaction with a telemarketer trying to get me interested in investing in an alpaca farm. Then came evening, and in due course, as is only natural, early night followed. And with this came the call.

This was not a typical call, as Simon explained to me, apologizing for the loud munching sounds coming over the phone line (he was devouring a high protein bar). Simon weighed about a hundred pounds, and you could probably see his ribs when he unveiled his trunk—I say probably because I've never seen (and have no desire to see) his bare chest. My point, in brief, is that if ever there was a man in need of good old carbohydrates, fats, and plenty of cholesterol, it was Simon, our expert forensic investigator.

But to return to the crime scene and its atypicality: Typically, when the medical examiner is called, there is a body. Here, there was no actual body *yet*, but it was presumed, very strongly indeed, that there *had* to be one on the other side of the door.

"It's George Zimaresh," Simon told me over the phone.

"What about him?"

"He's dead."

"Oh," I said. I've never been a fan of Zimaresh's bloody brand of detective fiction. Too much violence and not nearly intelligent enough. But he had sold millions of copies and had become a very wealthy man as a result.

"He's got to be dead, just got to be," said Simon.

"Why is it so spectacularly necessary for him to be dead?"

"There's a party going on at his house, and he was inside his study, and then the guests heard him screaming, *'Help, I'm going to be decapitated.'* There was another scream, and the guests tried to break into the room, but they couldn't. They called the police, and, well, you're the medical examiner for the night, and so you've got to be there too."

"I see," I said, feeling very low all of a sudden. I felt sorry for the poor man. I was in no mood to investigate this crime. I hadn't even eaten the drab pasta I'd microwaved. I hadn't seen a single drop of blood yet, and already, it sounded too gruesome.

"But listen," I said, "shouldn't we be calling someone else, like a real medical examiner? This seems like it's going to be a high-profile case. Maybe Spence? Or any of the other guys…" One of the other guys was actually a gal, and her name was Dr. Felicity Moon or Moon the Plastic Surgeon-Magnet. In the last five years, she'd been engaged to three different surgeons, all of them, peculiarly, plastic surgeons. But that wasn't the point; she was a damn good medical examiner, much better than I was, at any rate.

"There is no one, absolutely no one else who can come right this minute. Dr. Spence's not here, and Dr. Moon won't get in until early tomorrow morning."

3

We arrived separately at Zimaresh's house in the plush River Oaks area. An enormous oak tree spread its branches over the second floor of Zimaresh's three-story mansion. I felt unreasonably envious, but my envy was short-lived. After all, Zimaresh was no longer a man to be envied. He was dead (most likely), and I wasn't, and when you're dead, a mansion in River Oaks or any other exclusive neighborhood hardly matters. I felt several twinges of pity for this man. Life is something worth more than an infinite number of extraordinary houses. Life is more than money, but as people say, some lives do have a price upon them, as I was soon to discover.

I put on a fairly professional face, doing my best to look competent. But I was nowhere near to competence, of course. The last time I'd flitted anywhere near a real murder crime scene completely on my own was over a year ago, in dear old Potokapaw, home to a disproportionately high number of hideous crimes. And even then, when I'd been forced to put on the medical examiner hat, I'd always had backup. And luck had usually been on my side, and there were, in general, happy endings. But now I was in a big city, with big-city rules; a prominent Houstonian lay dead; and the paparazzi would be all over the place like maggots devouring a piece of rotten flesh.

Simon sensed my apprehension.

"Don't worry," he said, "I've done a lot of these."

He was right. I was there just for the show; the forensic investigator, in this case, Simon, was the real man of the moment. He'd gather the pertinent forensic evidence, I could be sure of it. He'd been doing this before I'd even been conceived, I'm sure of it. That put me in a better mood instantly.

"Cigarette?" he asked.

I was shocked. Some politically correct element inside me sprang up.

"I don't smoke," I said a bit stiffly.

"You can just roll the cigarette between your fingers. Dr. Moon does it. It makes you look more effective."

"Does she smoke?"

"Hell, no! She just rolls it between her fingers."

"I see." I thought about it. "Am I supposed to light it?"

"Not unless you want to smoke it," said Simon.

"Won't people realize that I'm not actually smoking it?"

"Hell, they'll have other things on their minds."

I resisted the temptation to ask: If they do have other things on their minds, then why on earth would they notice a stupid cigarette in my fingers? But we were now on the threshold of the house. The door was open, and I passed a couple of policemen inside. Interestingly, they did take note of my cigarette in my hand with what appeared to be appreciation. Maybe the cigarette mattered after all (I hope this doesn't sound like I'm stereotyping every cop everywhere…many of them, I am sure, hate the very sight of cigarettes).

4

People of all sizes and shapes, people looking like Napoleon Bonaparte, Cleopatra, Bill Clinton, and other famous personalities, and one guy who tried discreetly to stay out of the way. He was disguised as a condom, with his head poking out of the end. Totally tasteless, of course, but it was hard not to stare at him, even as he tried his best to avoid my gaze. I noticed some faces I'd seen in the newspapers, prominent persons all, dressed in all manner of disguises: priests, concubines, police officers, surgeons in their scrubs. I was looking at a Who's Who of Houston's rich and famous enjoying themselves at a costume party. They all looked like confused rabbits now, some with greater curiosity than others. An exception was one guy who was so drunk that he merely smiled and winked at me in a dizzy, drunken way. It was obvious that the recent happenings, a man screaming, then likely murdered, and so on, had made little impact on him—lucky devil. To pass through life not feeling any pain or worry, being totally out of it, does have some appealing points, doesn't it? (I came to know later that he was Art Morkins—and he was a mystery writer too, but not a well-known one. He was very rich, his family fortune somehow based on tomatoes. His greatest ambition in life was to become a second Agatha Christie. To this end, he had written and self-published many of his dreadful novels, including the ghastly *Murder on the Tallahassee Express*.)

I waded through a confusion of smells as well. There was, of course, the subtle aroma of exclusive, rich cologne mixed in with a vaster quantity of more pungent bouquets (probably some name-brand, ultra-expensive stuff). And yes, there was also an un-miss-able element of plain old sweat, quite a bit of it actually, because until only a short while ago, the rooms had been packed with dancing, gyrating, perspiring bodies (some of whom, in the normal course of events, might have ended up dancing, gyrating, perspiring in even closer proximity without any clothes as the night wore on. This may just be my overactive imagination. I am what you may call an inverse snob: I look down upon the rich, the famous, the successful; I see them as little better than dogs in heat, in the heat of power, wealth, and lust—*satisfied* lust, I should say. It's very likely that I am very wrong; I bet there are some good eggs mixed in with the foul lot. Naturally, I can't exclude the possibility that my snobbishness is a sour-grapes reaction to not being rich myself.).

Finally, I was standing facing the door of Zimaresh's study.

There must have been, I swear it, twenty or so police officers milling about. Short ones, tall ones, fat ones, thin ones. Virtually every single body type was represented in this bunch of officers. Some of them I couldn't imagine taking down a vicious killer; one guy looked so frail that I was afraid he would soon drop to the ground unless someone propped him up.

"We're going to have to break the door down," said a tall, big-boned woman with a long, angular, lean, attractive face. She was wearing plain clothes. "This place is like a zoo! Somebody—maybe several people at the party made many 911 calls. The entire police department seems to be here. Many more than we need, I hope…Lieutenant Helen Freud," she said, extending a hand to me.

"Freud," I repeated.

"I married into Freuds," she said, smiling. "But these Freuds are not related to the famous everything's-all-about-sex Freud, the one you're thinking of. We don't think of sex all the time, but we do have some now and then, much more *then* than *now*, if you get my drift. Things get very busy at times."

Here I was, getting a peep into the private sex life of Lieutenant Helen Freud; I shouldn't say private because she was declaring this publicly in a loud voice to a total stranger outside the door of a study where a man supposedly lay decapitated. None of the uniformed officers reacted to her remark with any surprise. I assumed from this that she was in the habit of broadcasting the secrets of the Freud bedroom.

All this would've been well under other circumstances, but we were just about to break an ornate door, probably worth a month's salary for me, to come upon and examine a decapitated corpse…but, and I'm surprised to admit it, I felt lighter following this exchange. I liked this woman. A case of instant-like. You know what I'm talking about, the kind of like that just comes upon you with no logical reason behind it.

The door was of a strange kind. It was very broad and long, and it did not have a flat surface, the kind you'd expect any reasonable door to have. Instead, it had a complicated design with projecting figures of lions, iguanas, a priest with a ponytail, three dogs, a pigeon, another bird that I did not recognize, and a schoolgirl who, on closer inspection, turned out to be a Scotsman. I suppose the door was an "artistic" door. It probably had a message for those who "get" art—I don't, as a rule, and so the door simply appeared hideous to me.

Helen Freud acquainted me with the more relevant portions of the door.

"There is no doorknob," she said. "You can only enter it by pushing it if it's open. You can't enter if it's locked. And you can't lock it from the outside. You can only lock it from the inside."

"Interesting," I said. "Any other way of getting out of this room?"

"Only this door, if Perkins is to be believed."

"Who's Perkins?"

"Zimaresh's butler; no, his valet or something. His personal assistant."

"But that makes no sense," I said, intrigued. "If, and let me get the facts straight, if someone was attacking Zimaresh, and Zimaresh was yelling that he was about to be decapitated, then it follows that there has to be another person in the room. And if there was another person, then that person could not leave the room without leaving the door unlocked.

And so if the door is locked, and there's no other way out of the room, then the decapitator, the killer, has to be inside."

"I couldn't have put it better myself. All we've got to do is to open the door. This is going to be an open-and-shut case if you'll pardon the pun."

"But shouldn't we be careful?" I said. "The murderer's probably armed, with a sword at least…"

"I wouldn't worry about that," said Freud. "We're armed to the teeth here too."

"Shouldn't we be reasoning with this murderer—trying to get him to open the door?"

"We've thought about that already. But it's a soundproof room. No sound gets in."

That struck me as odd, but I couldn't figure out why immediately.

"But you see, my guess is that whoever killed him is dead too."

"How so?"

"Well, it's obvious he's some kind of nut. He kills Zimaresh, then turns the weapon on himself." She paused and bellowed at the two men with the drill and electric saw. "Be careful with the door! I want the lock intact. I am totally into locks," she explained to me. "Oh, in a totally non-S&M sort of way," she guffawed, supplying me with more unnecessary info. "I have a professional interest in them. Plus, the lock of this door is material evidence."

The officers with the saw were drilling through the priest's belly button on the door, well clear of the "material evidence." Freud kept snapping at the two, though I'm certain that her snapping was totally unnecessary. They looked like the sort of men who could make their way through doors, even bizarre, valuable ones like this one, in their sleep, without any pep talks from her.

"We've got to move back," said Helen.

I obeyed. It was taking forever to cut a rectangle through the door. But it appeared that the job was about to be completed. If there was a homicidal maniac on the other side with a gun, then it was probably better to watch out. Being something of a coward and insanely in love with my life, I took a safe position behind an enormous plant and became practically invisible to the human eye.

"Oh, there you are, behind the tree. Good idea." Freud took several steps back to where I was to inspect my hiding place. "This is one hell of a house plant," she said.

"I agree. Enormous."

It was enormous—and ghastly. I don't know who Zimaresh's interior decorator was. I'd have advised him against the plant. A brown trunk so broad that two people could have easily hidden behind it or even inside it; and green, shiny, plastic leaves that arched over my head. All in all, it was a horrible addition to any room.

"It's got a funny smell," said Freud.

"I know," I said. "Plastic or poly-something."

Our attention was distracted by a police officer waving to Freud.

"We're ready," he said.

The officers pushed the rectangle down, stepping away from the aperture. I retreated further behind the plant.

"It's strictly routine from this point on—at least I hope," said Freud.

I didn't ask what "routine" was. Did it mean homicidal maniacs shooting bullets at you?

Judging from the three officers with their bulletproof vests and some kind of contraption covering their faces, I sensed that there was potential for the situation to take a sudden southward turn into chaos.

"Here's where I come into the picture," said Freud. Grabbing a megaphone from a creature who looked like a prototypical lackey, she announced:

"TURN YOURSELF IN OR WE'LL BE FORCED TO SHOOT AT YOU.

"How'd that sound?" She turned to me.

The lackey, a thin slip of a man who was a kind of shadow to Helen Freud (he was so constantly by her side that I kept forgetting he was there), nodded enthusiastically. "Should get him out in no time," he said in a voice that was throaty and barely audible but obviously congratulatory.

"People don't think I mean business just because I'm a girl."

A lot of girl, I thought. She was tall and loomed over the scene in complete control. No one was likely to mess with her.

The next few minutes were silent. No volley of bullets, no mad screaming of a demented murderer waving a sword, nothing.

Helen Freud was looking through the hole into the room.

"Doctor," she said, sounding different, more serious, "you'd better take a look at this."

5

Before I could get inside, however, we had to make sure that there wasn't a killer inside the room. The spacious study was soon crawling with police officers—as I said before, there must have been at least twenty or so—maybe more. One of the most important things in a crime scene is to keep the scene as "clean" as possible—you can't have dozens of people trampling in like mad elephants. But in this case, the situation was different. There was somebody armed on the other side—or so we assumed. The vested police officers—I mean those who were covered up—went in first, and they were followed by the others. The situation was completely chaotic and rapidly out of control—forget about keeping the scene pristine. Everywhere you turned, there was a police officer. But it was a huge room. There could've been twenty more cops, and it still wouldn't feel cramped inside.

But after a short while of cops poking here and there, it became apparent that there was no one inside the room. No one except for the man in the tux. A man without a head, I should say, in a plush chair. The neck wound was moist with deep-red blood. In fact, in order to get to the body, we had to walk *splotch-splotch* through his blood. Recall that the average amount of blood in a human body is five liters, and practically all of the five liters or so that he had in life was now on the carpeted floor, and you may get an approximate idea of how messy it was. I say approximate because there is no way to imagine or describe a scene such as this. My joggers squished through the blood-drenched carpet, and I could feel the wetness, even through my socks and shoes—as if I was wading through flood-soaked mud. A very unpleasant sensation.

The smell of blood saturated the atmosphere inside the room. For those of you who've never smelled blood, here's a word of advice: Don't.

As often as you can, avoid situations where you'll be forced to inhale the metallic, fleshy odor of blood.

The police officers were going over the large room like bees checking out the tastiest flowers. But they kept a respectful distance from me. In fact, in a few moments, there was an uncomfortable silence in the room. And I realized that all eyes were upon me. I was the medical examiner, the expert, the one who was supposed to get all over the headless body and make profound forensic remarks…at least, that's what I've come to expect from TV shows and detective novels and also from experienced forensic pathologists, and I was (and am) neither. I have no objective way of knowing this, but I suppose that I appeared a bit of a bumbling idiot, standing there with my mouth open. The first order of business was to shut my gaping mouth and to twist it, assuming a frown, a thoughtful frown. I carefully avoided meeting anyone's gaze by acquiring what's called a "faraway" look in my eyes. I took short, purposeful steps toward the headless victim. I surveyed the wound. It was fairly smooth, so I imagined that the stroke had been a swift one, with a sharp, heavy sword slicing through the soft tissues and the intervertebral disc in one rapid motion. An intervertebral disc is the tissue that cushions the space between the bones of the neck. If the sword had struck any of the neck bones, the vertebrae, it wouldn't have cut straight through—because these bones are extremely hard; the killer would've had to strike a second time.

"Interesting," I muttered.

Freud was all over me like a bloodhound catching an intoxicating scent. "What? What's interesting?"

"The wound is so smooth."

"And?"

"Well, it could be chance, of course," I said, sounding exactly like an expert. "The killer struck the victim, who isn't tied or anything, and got the head off in one clean sweep."

"I see what you're saying…" said Freud with palpable excitement in her voice. Unlike me, she clearly thrived in abnormal, violent situations. "It's as if Mr. Zimaresh was cooperating with his killer."

"Exactly," I said.

"Which makes no sense," said Freud, "since he was screaming and yelling and was trying to get away."

"My guess is," I reasoned, using no forensic knowledge but plain common sense, "that he was sitting on this chair, ready for the chop. The killer comes from behind, marks the spot somehow, maybe with his fingers, between the vertebrae—I mean the neck bones—and goes for it with his sword."

"Hmm," said Freud. "And that's absurd, right? I mean, why would he be sitting in a chair, letting someone mark the spot, waiting to be decapitated?" She wondered aloud.

"There's something even more strange," I said, suddenly realizing why the screaming, yelling business was all wrong. "Everyone heard him shouting for his life, right?"

Freud nodded.

"But how is that possible if this was a soundproof room? No one should've been able to hear anything."

"You're right, of course," said Freud, delivering a sudden slap on my back, almost knocking me over into the victim's bloody lap. "Brilliant, Holmes!"

"Oh please," I said, feigning false modesty. Actually, I was quite pleased with my extremely elementary deduction. It was, I'll admit, nowhere near Holmes, or Poirot, or Miss Marple, or any of those brilliant fictional detectives. But I was a real-life human being, fairly average, and so the occasional exercise of common sense made me feel quite brilliant. It takes very little to satisfy mere mortals like myself. Holmes or Hercule Poirot could have figured it all out by now, but I had to take baby steps, fetal or embryonic steps, to be more accurate.

But I was warming to another, rather obvious observation.

"If there's a body, there must be a head. Where's the head?"

Freud added: "Yes, and question number two: where's the weapon? Question number three, where's the murderer? If there's no way out of this room, then where did the killer disappear? Unless Mr. Zimaresh somehow decapitated himself and then managed to make the murder weapon and his own head disappear…"

It was truly as unbelievable as those unbelievable crimes that mystery writers come up with in book after book.

There had to be a perfectly clear, rational, physical explanation. The assassin killed his victim, then left the room, somehow locking the door behind him or her, even though this was precisely something he or she couldn't have done. But the killer had to have done it, and if we all thought very hard, maybe we would figure out how…

"Why didn't he leave the head behind?" asked Freud.

Why was she asking me? She was probing me with her wide eyes. I think she imagined (incorrectly) that I might be able to shed some light on the process. I couldn't and told her so fairly quickly.

"I haven't a clue. We may need a forensic psychiatrist. It may mean something in psycho terms. Maybe our killer collects heads—as trophies," I said.

At this point, Simon let out a small burp. Judging from the blush that spread over his wrinkled face, this was evidently not his intention. Perhaps he had meant to cough discreetly to catch our attention. Embarrassingly for him, the cough had been poorly executed, ending up as a fairly typical, short, but exceedingly loud belch.

"That'd be Dr. Wainsworth. He's the forensic psychiatrist," he said. "Excuse me."

"Too many beans, eh?" Freud laughed, nudging him in the ribs. Trust her not to ignore a social misfire.

"Where's Dr. Wainsworth?" I asked.

"He's in Paris. At an International Abnormal Psychopath conference."

"So that means there must be some *normal* psychopaths somewhere." Very abruptly, Freud became serious. "It's impossible," she said, repeating the obvious.

Yes, impossible.

A headless man.

No head.

No weapon.

And no way for the murderer to leave the room.

"He may've hidden the head somewhere," said Freud.

"The murderer's got to be inside the room," I said, feeling a chill. But even as I said it, I couldn't believe it. There was no murderer inside the room—or was there? If he was, where was he?

"I don't see a murderer," said Freud.

The room had a pentagonal desk table and chair in the center. This was evidently Zimaresh's workplace. This was where he churned out his best-selling non-masterpieces year after year. There was a computer, a PC, with an enormous screen, almost as large as my TV set.

Zimaresh had been sitting in his writing chair, one with wheels, the kind that can rotate. He had probably been swung around so that he was facing the door when we entered.

"It's like he's on display," I said to no one in particular.

This is the problem with reading too many mystery novels, like I do. You start seeing angles and plots in the smallest of occurrences.

But it seemed that I had a good probability of being right.

I said to Helen Freud:

"Let us suppose our murderer wants to decapitate Zimaresh."

"Supposed—then what?" said Freud, rubbing her chin.

"It is unlikely that he would have gotten between the chair and the desk. As you can see, the chair is almost touching the desk. So he was killed somewhere else in the room, then brought right here, next to the desk, and the chair rotated so that he was facing us when we entered the room."

"I see what you mean," said Freud. "On display."

"The killer's got to be a psychopath of some kind."

Freud was examining the desk.

"No blood on the desk," she said. "Not a drop."

She stopped as if very surprised.

"Now, what do we have here?" she barked with energy.

I saw what she had picked up from the desk.

An envelope.

A sealed envelope.

The most interesting, I should say amazing, thing about this envelope was what it said on the back of it in bold capital letters,

FOR DR. IMOGENE CHAPLIN

6

FOR DR. IMOGENE CHAPLIN...

My surprise was the same as if someone had just burst onto the scene and announced that after a freak, impromptu election, I had suddenly and unanimously been elected the President of the United States.

Of course, now that I look back upon it, it makes perfect sense. But it didn't then. It made anything but sense.

Helen Freud was gazing—no staring—at me.

"Did you know George Zimaresh?" she asked.

"Know him? No, of course not. I can't figure out why he'd be writing letters to me."

"But he has," said Freud stubbornly.

"Yes, I am aware that he has. May I see it?"

"Only if I get to read it too," said Freud, very seriously, and then almost immediately burst into a laugh.

Well, really! From where I stood, this was no laughing matter. A freshly beheaded individual had left a note for me—a total stranger. I didn't know how I felt: a little worried, perhaps, but why was I worried? It's not as if I was somehow connected to this strange crime. But that wasn't true—I was *definitely* connected to this strange crime! The letter proved it, didn't it?

After a seemingly interminable delay, the envelope was opened.

The letter was typed.

Dear Imogene (it said),

I hope you don't mind me calling you by your first name. After all, I am writing this, one of the very last things I will ever write, to you, and in the last few weeks, I feel *that I've come to know you rather well. It's a pity we never had a chance to be intimate, though I assure you that you would have found an experience with me to be quite phenomenal and exhilarating. You may care to check out testimonials in that regard, if you like. In the top left-hand drawer, you will find a little green book (I find the convention of a little <u>black</u> book quite tiresome, don't you agree?). In this book, you will find the names of all my—I hate to use the word—<u>conquests</u>, but I assure you all these conquests of mine yielded to me not only willingly but enthusiastically.*

Now you are wondering why I write this to you, isn't that so? You are asking yourself, "I am Imogene Chaplin, a simple pathologist from Potokapaw, and I've never met the great George Zimaresh. Why, then, is he writing this letter to me?" Well, this is what we call a <u>clue</u> in the mystery world. Figure out the answer to this one, and you will have figured out the <u>seventh</u> clue I have left for you.

Now you're probably asking yourself: "Hmmm…seventh clue—what about the first six?"

Now Imogene, you can't expect me to tell you everything, do you? You don't want me to suck all the mystery out of this, do you? Ahhh, the joy of being alive and being able to solve a good mystery. It is something I shall never have any more, I'm sorry to say, being so very dead at the time you read this letter.

But, because I realize that you're an ordinary mortal and not an especially brilliant one at that, and because I really want you to solve this mystery, I am not going to leave you clueless. I'll tell you a few of the clues. Figuring them out should still keep your hands full. How's that for a deal?

Here are some of the clues, presented to you roughly in the order in which you might encounter them:

Number one: The incredible number of police officers. I'll bet there are a lot of them, no?

Number two: The tree outside my writing room. I always hated it, but it has a function.

Number three: The absence of my head.

Number four: The absence of a weapon or my assailant—who only did what I asked him to, good man!

Number five: The blood—quite a bit of it, wouldn't you agree?

Number six: For you to figure out.

Number seven: I already told you: This letter (and others) that I have written to you, which you will receive in due course.

Number eight: The tree. I hope you haven't been distracted by my headless corpse to notice that there is an identical tree in the room.

Number nine: A question for you: Is there any way out of this room other than through this door? So that you don't go crazy trying to answer this one, may I recommend Perkins to you? He's my trusted valet and very well-informed.

This will have to do for the time being. I've left instructions for you to keep getting mail from me at appropriately timed intervals, with more clues, ideas, hints, just like in a mystery in a book.

If there were any justice in this world, I'd be around to write this real-life mystery of my suicide. It could have been the best thing I ever wrote. Somebody else could do it, maybe? What about you? No, just kidding.

I would love to just sit and keep on writing to you, but you hardly know me, and you might think strangely of me if the letter got to be too long. So I will end here wishing you with all my heart: good hunting.

By the way, I've e-mailed a copy of this letter to our local and national newspapers. So don't be surprised if you are hounded by reporters. Who knows, you may get to like the attention.

Don't let yourself get bored,

George Zimaresh

I looked blankly at Freud.

"The guy was a nutcase," I said.

"Agreed," said Freud.

"Has he really committed suicide, or is he playing…some kind of horrible practical joke?"

"Well," said Freud, "Without getting too technical about it, this doesn't look like a suicide—he couldn't have decapitated himself, then hidden both the weapon and his head—such a thing is, as I'm sure you'll agree, an impossibility. He could've commissioned a suicide; got somebody else to do it—but in that case, what happened to this other person?"

"But how do we know it's him?" I asked. "The head is missing. Why is it missing? One reason could be that Zimaresh was crazy. Another could be that this dead man *is not really Zimaresh but someone else*. And the head has been removed to fool us into believing—incorrectly—that this person is Zimaresh."

"Possible," said Freud. "But I think you've been reading too many detective novels; the truth is a lot less complicated than those damn fool mystery writers make it out to be. Anyway, I can't debate this now. You can go all over the body at your leisure and make sure it's him—or not. At the moment, the clues in his letter may be a good place to start. May I see the letter, please?"

7

Number one: The incredible number of police officers. I'll bet there's a lot of them, no?

Clue number one was meaningless to us. Yes, there were too many police officers. They were everywhere, even though by now, they had re-treated away from the center of the room, giving us space to do our job. You know how it is in traffic accidents or emergencies; all of a sudden, there are a lot of cops everywhere. In this case, we were aware that some-one—likely many people had made many emergency 911 calls. This ac-counted for their presence. How was that a clue to anything?

"My guess is," said Freud, "That this guy is just showing off. He's a mystery writer who makes his living writing silly books about impossible crimes that could never happen in real life. I mean, like this crime. This is a detective-story crime, don't you get that feeling? Totally made up and pointless and of no value to anyone except the writer who gets to make big bucks out of it."

I resisted the impulse to say that I, for one, found detective stories entertaining, and so they were of value to me (at least). So what if the crimes in most mystery stories could never have happened in real life? I think it's a blessing that life's not really like what mystery writers make it out to be.

Freud went on:

"So, he's daring us. Zimaresh didn't or doesn't care how many police officers there are; in fact, the more there are, the better. It's all about the drama for him. So, he's staged his own suicide—"

"Or somebody else's murder," I muttered, but not softly enough. I caught Freud's half-irritated glare at me.

"He's staged his own suicide, or somebody else's murder, as our forensic examiner points out," she said. "He wants as many police officers as he can get."

"But how is that a clue?" I asked.

"I haven't a clue," said Freud, unexpectedly letting out a loud belch-like laugh.

Really, I thought, most un-lady-like, but that is precisely what I liked about this woman.

"So, onto clue number two," said Freud, and read, "*Number two: The tree outside my writing room. I always hated it, but it has a function.*"

This was something less obscure.

"The tree is large enough to hold a man—maybe the killer," said Freud.

We were soon outside the room, circling around and examining the monstrosity.   The trunk was broad—exceedingly broad indeed. Was it hollow?

Freud rapped on the leathery brown covering of the tree. There was a *boing-boing* sound as if it were hollow.

"Hmmm," she said.

She felt it along its length. At one point, she was practically embracing the wide trunk.

The tree was no help at all.

"I'm not getting anywhere," she spat out in obvious irritation. "Where's the housekeeper?"

There was a discreet cough.

Beyond the perimeter of the yellow police DO NOT CROSS tape, there stood an inconspicuous fellow wearing horn-rimmed glasses.

"Possibly you mean the valet," he said in a refined, British-sounding voice.

"I mean, whoever can help me with this here tree,"

"That would be the valet, madam. I am referring to myself."

"Well, come on here, then, what's your name?"

"That would be Perkins, madam, at your service," he said, hopping over the police tape in the most dignified way imaginable. He held it down with one finger and gradually brought first his right foot and then the left. We watched quietly as he performed this maneuver, which certainly took longer than it should have. As he walked past me, I got the whiff of a pleasant-smelling cologne. I also got a closer look at him. He was dark and at least past fifty, not as young as he had appeared from a distance.

"It's a simple device," he said, bending at his knees so that he was level with the middle of the trunk. "You have to feel it with your fingers because it's not visible," he explained.

"*What* is not visible?" asked Freud.

"Something in the nature of a button—in point of fact, exactly a button, but cleverly concealed within the folds of the artificial bark of this tree. You press it like so, and the trunk opens."

Something snapped, and a part of the trunk came unstuck. It was like a curved door.

He hooked his fingers around this door and opened it.

He stepped back, pleased at the results.

Freud let out a whistle.

8

The inside of the trunk was indeed broad enough to admit two not-too-obese individuals. What's more, there were steps leading down underground from the center.

"Where the hell do these steps go?"

"To the other tree, the one inside the study," said Perkins. "Mr. Zimaresh was fond of playing jokes on his guests. If you will note there are bookshelves behind the inside tree; Mr. Zimaresh would pretend to browse through the books, step into the inside tree, which is identical to this one, go down the stairs, which go under the room, enter the outside tree, exit the outside tree, emerge on the other side of the door which would be locked, of course, knock on the door. The guest would open the door, typically shrieking with amazement."

"All women, these friends, right?" Freud asked

"However did you guess?"

"You said, 'shrieking with amazement.' Not many men shriek with amazement."

"Quite so. There might be some who do, but Mr. Zimaresh preferred shriekers of the female gender."

"I see," said Freud. "Well, that explains how the murderer was able to escape. He went into the tree—the inside tree—went down the steps, and left by the outside tree. He escaped before we got here."

"Oh, I would say that's highly unlikely, if not downright impossible," said Perkins.

Freud gawked at him.

"Why in God's name is that impossible?"

"Oh, for a very simple reason, madam. You see, there is a peculiarity in the way the trapdoors in these trees are designed. They can only be locked from the inside but can be unlocked either from the inside or from the outside. As you observed, the trapdoor of this tree was shut; I had to press the button to unlock it. If the murderer had left by way of the tree, the door would've been open, precluding my need to unlock it."

Freud absorbed this information.

"So what you're telling me is that a guy can't exit this tree and lock the tree trap door from the outside."

"Exactly. That would be impossible."

"But if that's the case," Freud exclaimed, "Then we must examine the other tree at once."

We were back at the other tree, like inquisitive children. The other tree's "door" was open. Freud opened it wide without having to press any button.

"So, Perkins, let me see if I understand this tree business. At any given time, only one tree trapdoor can be locked."

"That would be correct, madam, unless you decided to stay inside and never came out. But that would be unlikely. When you enter a tree, you have the option of locking it from the inside by operating a latch—this is the latch that the button unhooks or unlatches," he said, fingering the latch almost lovingly. "But in order to emerge out of the other tree or even the same tree, you have to open the trapdoor of that tree; when you do so, the door is, obviously, no longer locked."

"But surely, when you first got these trees, they both *had* to be locked."

"I'm afraid I don't see why," said Perkins with an expression of suffering and pain on his face. He continued snobbishly, "Mr. Zimaresh did not acquire these in a department store where everything is packaged and locked when you take it out of its wrapper. He had these constructed, specifically. It took nearly a month to construct the two trees, the steps, and the underground tunnel connecting the trees. As you may imagine, this enterprise cost an enormous amount of money." He opened his mouth as if to say more but stopped and looked straight into Helen Freud's eyes.

I don't know if Freud noticed that he hadn't said everything he could've said. She was on to her next question:

"Why did he have this stuff built?"

"He was working on a manuscript."

"What kind of manuscript?"

"It was supposed to be a classic locked room mystery in the grand detective tradition."

"Well, did he finish it?"

Perkins sighed, "Afraid not, madam. Truth be told, I was rather keen to read it. But he ran into some problems with it. I remember him telling me that locked room mysteries were difficult to write believably. Nobody could do a locked room murder in real life, he told me. The trouble was that he wanted to write a perfect locked room murder mystery that could easily happen in real life."

"Interesting," said Freud, licking her lips. "Can you tell me something more about this thing he was writing?"

"I'm afraid not, madam. Mr. Zimaresh was very secretive about his work. He was superstitious and believed that if he spoke too much about your novel, the inspiration would vanish, and he would be left with nothing. He once said to me, and I quote, 'A novel talked about before it is complete is like a virgin who has had sex, or not really a virgin.'"

"But surely he has a copy of this novel of his sitting somewhere?" Freud persisted.

"Unquestionably. But I don't know where." Again, he opened his mouth as if to say something but then stopped. Freud looked at him sharply, with a quizzical expression on her face, as if she was trying to read Perkins's thoughts. But Perkins had a smooth look, unreadable.

"Are you *sure* you don't know," she pressed him.

Perkins stiffened, "Perhaps his publisher might know."

Everything happens all at once in situations like these, I mean, a murder case. People are either all over the place, doing this or that, or gather around someone, or just wandering around aimlessly, feeling and looking confused. As I've mentioned about a hundred times, I fit into the "confused" category, but not because I didn't know what to do. My job was comparatively easy. I had a corpse, the corpse was headless, and so the cause of death was no mystery. What remained was to try and gather useful forensic evidence helpful in finding who'd done it to whom. Luckily for me, that's where a skilled forensic investigator comes in especially handy. Simon was just such a guy, and so I let him attend to the forensic evidence—it's always best to leave such things to experts. Basically, that left me with little to do but hang around, looking (I hoped) intelligent. But like I said, I was bewildered about many things, and I think that my bewilderment was obvious to all.

For example, let's consider Perkins. I found him confusing—or, I should say, difficult to understand. Here was a man whose employer had just been beheaded. Most people would find such a happening catastrophic and jarring. Some might get hysterical. Or become very quiet. Or something. But not Perkins. He was a model of normality. His behavior was refined, composed, and proper. The only thing ruffled about him was his hair, briefly, which became quite messy at one point in time; he had gotten it out of order after tripping on something shortly after crossing the DO NOT CROSS police tape. He was helped to his feet by Helen's assistant. Perkins saw me staring at him, then raised his eyes and quickly adjusted his hair. He nodded to me as if thanking me for pointing out his less-than-perfect hair. You get the idea of what Perkins was like, don't you? This is exactly the sort of thing they teach in valet school. Maybe they get lessons on how to remain calm and professional when your boss has been decapitated.

I looked at him again. He had suddenly become very still. I could see that he was puzzled, as if struck by a momentous thought. He was so distracted by this thought that he missed Freud's next question to him about the name of the publisher. She had to ask him a second time before he answered.

When I look back, I realize I had missed a very important clue: the clue to the whole business. It was right there in front of my face, but I wasn't looking for it. Just like in a detective novel, except that this was not a story but real life unfolding before me. Before this drama finished unfolding, there would be much trouble. Alas, had I but understood what I had seen, maybe the whole sorry saga could have been finished then and there or sooner than it did.

But I paid no attention to this valuable clue, the most valuable one really, the solution to the whole problem. Sometimes, I think I was quite a fool, but I hope that you will agree with me when I say that the clue was not easy to spot. It was only later, when I pieced the whole thing together, that the thing fell in place. But I am distracting you with all this. I will let the events speak for themselves, just as they happened, and let you decide if I had been really so stupid to have missed something so obvious.

To return to the clues of the trees:

Freud said,

"Bottom line: the outside tree door is closed, the inside one is open. Point number two: the trees, like this damn door, only lock from the *inside*. What does that mean? How's that a clue?"

There followed a silence punctuated only by the soft sounds of Simon squatting on the floor, collecting blood from the floor into a tube.

Surprisingly, it was Perkins who answered. I say "surprisingly" because it is customary for witnesses to remain as mute and invisible as possible in these situations. The idea is: lie low or hidden so the police forget about you; the thing to do, if you're a witness or a possible suspect, is to do your best to avoid the police. I can't say I blame people for being like this. Any time I hear a police siren while I'm driving, I always instinctively conclude that I've done something terribly wrong and slow down guiltily.

People are afraid of the police, maybe because everyone has something to feel guilty about.

But Perkins was clearly enjoying himself now, even though he was careful to let no trace of emotion creep into his even tone.

"I may be able to provide something in the nature of an answer. I may be wrong, but I have an idea of how Mr. Zimaresh's mind worked. Naturally, I can't presume to be as brilliant as he was, but I recall, at this time, his 'The Case of the Golden Slipper.' This was a complicated story, almost as good as something Agatha Christie or Arthur Conan Doyle might have written. In the interest of time, I am unable to summarize the whole tale before you, but I can tell you the crucial point in the story. In this story, the golden slipper was a clue to the crime, but it was a clue by *not* being present where it should have been. The connection with the clue of the two trees may be as follows: the inside tree was open, and the outside tree was not, exactly the opposite of what you'd have expected. So, the clue is: the killer did not leave through the trees, by way of the outside tree, because the outside tree is closed."

"I see," said Freud, looking with great suspicion at Perkins. "And you just figured this out?"

Her tone was a bit threatening, a tad dangerous, as if she was strongly contemplating clobbering the little man.

But Perkins was not shaken. Looking at him, I half-wished I could have gone to valet school. Then, I, too, would be stronger, more in control, able to keep my cool in difficult circumstances.

"I would love to claim that I did, but the truth is, no. I did not just figure this out. I had a hint——"

"A hint? From whom?"

"From Mr. Zimaresh, of course."

9

There was the kind of silence that writers like to call a stunned silence. You know what I mean. Something happens, and everything comes to a complete halt, with people gawking like idiots.

The effect on Freud was electric. She went a deep red and looked about ready to explode. Perkins sensed that he couldn't just say something like "From Mr. Zimaresh, of course," and leave it at that. Such a statement was hazardous to the man's continued state of good health.

He said quickly, "I see by your expression that you desire greater detail in response to your question. Mr. Zimaresh had hinted to me yesterday that something significant might happen today and had urged me to read his collection of short stories, *A Random Collection of Sex and Murder*. This is the collection that includes *The Case of the Golden Slipper*, the one I alluded to. I read the story and drew the obvious conclusion. The closed outside tree door is like the golden slipper that isn't where it's supposed to be."

Freud appeared to cool down a little.

"Do you know any more about this?"

"I don't know what you're referring to, madam."

"What am I referring to? Why damn it, man, what the hell do you think I'm referring to! I'm referring to your dead, decapitated boss, that's who I am referring to. What do you know about this?"

"I fear I *don't* know any more than I *do* know, which is not much. It appears that Mr. Zimaresh decided to end his life and thought of an unusual way of doing so. I can only tell you that this sort of behavior, though bizarre to an outsider, is fairly typical of Mr. Zimaresh. He was ever fond of playing tricks and practical jokes, and while his present trick is unusual even by his standards, I don't put it past him. I imagine he thought he would exit life while putting on a damn good show, madam, for the benefit of the audience. It was his mission, madam, to place entertainment and enjoyment in the hands of his readers. His readers sensed that. They knew he was out to please them, to divert their minds from life's real and pressing problems. There were no deep, mystical, or philosophical meanings buried inside his novels. He liked to amuse, to puzzle, and to mystify people. In answer to your inevitable next question, I can't imagine what drove him to the extreme of planning his own death in this manner."

Freud was not finished with him, however.

"And you feel nothing, no sense of grief or shock?"

"I actually do feel grief. I feel terribly sad," he said gravely. "I wish he hadn't decided to go this way. He was a very amusing man, very entertaining, and a kind and splendid employer—I shall miss him. But I don't go about broadcasting my emotions. That is not what I'm paid for. My job is to serve and to serve without drawing attention to myself. I can't very well go around wailing and beating my chest, can I, even if it is to satisfy someone like you, who demands a more obvious display of grief."

These remarks had little or no effect on Freud. She looked as suspicious as ever. It was clear that she felt that Perkins knew something he wasn't telling us.

I felt the same. I kept thinking about the way he had been suddenly surprised. Had he seen something?

Like I said, here was the answer to everything, and I missed it. Oh well.

Freud worked her way down the list of clues.

"Number three: the absence of my head," she read.

"Here's my take on this clue," she announced to me, I imagine, since I was the only one who wasn't doing much but was just hanging around, kind of stunned by the circumstances (I confess: I am one of those who take a long time to adapt to unusual circumstances. It was still too soon for me to return to a state of normalcy. The situation was, as the expression goes, "far out"). The criminal investigators who work for the police department were gathering their clues—you know, things like fingerprints, combing for things like hairs, fibers, and so on, while Simon, my forensic investigator, was busy working with the body and the blood, gathering as much information as he could. One of his less enviable tasks was sticking a long rectal thermometer up the dead man's you-know-where (in order to help determine the time since death. In my limited experience, this really doesn't help that much in real life, no matter how easy it is made to sound in detective fiction). He was assisted in the process not by me but by one of the police investigators. Simon, as I've already mentioned, had collected whatever blood he needed for the lab tests.

"The clues about the lack of a head and the lack of a weapon: these are the same kinds of clues, at least in my opinion." She gave me a piercing look. "Why no head? Because this guy was a writer, full of drama, and he wanted to give this case a touch of mystery. Why no weapon? Same reason. Make it look impossible. Make us think. The guy was obviously crazy, but there you have it."

She gave me another piercing look. I think she sensed that I disagreed with her. I did in part, but I wasn't planning on opening my mouth to tell her so—not immediately anyway.

"You're not saying anything," she said to me. "OK. Out with it. What're your thoughts on the subject?"

"I think you may have a point," I began diplomatically. "But there might be an alternative explanation. I agree that the absence of the head may have to do with a crazy sense of the dramatic. But it's as if somebody's trying to hide the fact that this body doesn't really belong to Mr. Zimaresh. I mean, it's fantastic, isn't it? I mean, unless he was really insane, nobody plans his own death with, with, with so much, so much cheerfulness, right? I mean, read the letter, and you get the feeling he's not having too much of a bad time. Which is just, too, too, too odd for words. As to why there is no murderer or weapon: well, I think you're right. It is to make it seem impossible for us, like you said. I mean, it's *not* impossible because it really *happened* and was therefore *possible* in some way—we do have a dead man here, without a head, and no way anybody could've left the room carrying a head with him—or her—but somebody had to nevertheless, and we just missed it."

"I don't miss nothing like that," said Helen. "I—"

She was interrupted by a police officer. He pointed to something, and Freud followed him.

Needless to say, I followed Freud part of the way, stopping where Simon was but keeping Freud and the other officer in full view.

He—I mean the police officer—pointed to the telephone on the desk next to the desktop computer. Helen Freud picked up the phone, jabbed at one of the buttons, and said,

"TESTING ONE TWO THREE, JUST A TEST."

I jumped. I wasn't expecting her to sound quite so loud.

Then she made another announcement, "HELP, I'M BEING DECAPITATED."

"A public announcement system," said Freud, shaking her head. "So this is how Zimaresh got everyone's attention from this soundproof room. Proves my point. He allows himself to be decapitated but makes sure that people at his party know it. He had to get the police here for the show."

11

The fifth clue.

Freud held Zimaresh's letter towards me: "This clue is in your field. *Number five: The blood—quite a bit of it, wouldn't you agree?* Well, what do you expect? You cut off a man's head, man's got to bleed, right?"

"Right. So that can't be the clue unless it's a clue that tells us that he's been freshly decapitated. Maybe he's telling us when the murder took place. I mean, this guy—whoever he is—could have been killed earlier, maybe hours ago, and moved here—"

"From where? And once the murderer brought him in, how did he leave the room and lock it from the inside? It's the same problem whether he kills him before and moves him in later or kills him just a little while ago—either way, he's got to leave the room. You haven't seen the murderer leave the room, have you? So how'd he do it?"

I was thoughtful.

Yes, the problem remained the same. The murderer had obviously succeeded in leaving the room. And nobody had seen this guy leave the room, right?

"I don't know what the blood clue means. Simon's collecting it for analysis. Maybe that'll tell us something."

Yes, there was a lot of blood—we were sloshing about in a whole lot of blood. Much blood

Something struck me as funny about the blood. I tried unsuccessfully to put my finger on it but couldn't. It didn't fit somehow.

All this blood. *All this blood.* What was it about all this blood on the floor? The victim had pumped out nearly all of his five or so liters of blood on the floor through the neck wound. That's why there was all this blood on this floor. So why didn't it seem right?

I shook my head. A little later, the significance of this clue would surface, but I had to wait while my brain digested this morsel of a clue.

I didn't have much leisure time to spend thinking this through. Freud was charging, full speed, at the next clue.

"Now, what the hell kind of clue is this? *Number six: for you to figure out.*"

Freud mulled over the letter again, then handed it to me.

"Here, see if you can make any sense of it."

I read the letter again. After fifty seconds or so of intense concentration, I felt a throbbing sensation in my skull. Thinking hard does that to me sometimes. I usually stop thinking immediately, generally with good results.

"Well, you're no help!" Freud said half-jokingly, slapping me in the back.

12

Clue number seven (*Number seven: I already told you: This letter (and others) that I have written to you, which you will receive in due course.*), well, we didn't waste any time over that. Not beyond concluding that there was no clear reason why Zimaresh had succumbed to the desire to communicate with me, someone he couldn't possibly have known (but clearly did!). So, if it was a clue, maybe we'd have to get Perkins in again to try and figure this out. At any rate, Freud decided that it was unprofitable to mull over it at that time.

Clue number eight was about the inside tree. (*Number eight: The tree. I hope you haven't been distracted by my headless corpse to notice that there is an identical tree in the room.*) Freud was of the opinion that the tree business had been adequately dealt with. "Not the tree again!" she groaned, faking a realistic yawn, "Enough already!"

Finally, we came to clue number nine. (*Number nine: A question for you: Is there any way out of this room other than through this door? So that you don't go crazy trying to answer this one, may I recommend Perkins to you? He's my trusted valet and very well-informed*). We had shown that nobody could've left through the trees. This meant that there was yet another way out of the room.

This meant that it was time to haul good old Perkins back into the scene of the crime.

13

Rich writers, or rich people in general, can do things that mere mortals cannot even begin to imagine. Take George Zimaresh as an example. The man must have spent a fortune creating those dreadful trees for the sake of practical jokes and a book that he never even finished. And, as Perkins showed us, there was yet another way out of the room, except that it wasn't really a way out.

Zimaresh's study was surrounded by bookshelves with, I don't know, probably thousands of books. These were books by all the standard favorites of mystery readers the world over—Agatha Christie, Doyle, P.D. James, Ruth Rendell, Patricia Cornwell, John Sanford—if some guy or guy*ess* ever wrote a mystery, chances are you'd find it in Zimaresh's library. I have zero doubts that he borrowed ideas from the greats: I suppose it is inevitable to avoid doing so. I mean, there's only so much mystery you can create, and after a while, all the good plots are used up by the hundreds of mystery writers who write book after book after book. If I were a mystery writer, I guarantee you I'd be reading every mystery I could lay my hands on in the hopes of finding a terrific idea that I could "adapt" and pass off as my own.

But I'm going off on a tangent now, getting distracted as usual. Let me tell you about the bookshelves, in particular the ones next to a big bust of Agatha Christie on the west side of the study. This was something right out of tales of intrigue and unbelievable. You remove a book from the bookshelf, and the whole shelf moves back or rotates or something, and you find yourself staring into a secret passage. This is the kind of contraption that Zimaresh had designed.

The book you had to remove from the shelf was a hardback version of G.K. Chesterton's *The Complete Father Brown.* I remember reading

Chesterton's Father Brown mysteries when I was a teenager—but what I'd read I'd long forgotten (this may have been a coincidence. Father Brown would surface again when I spoke to my father the following day, but I'll get to that). Anyway, the passage—

It was broad, as broad, in fact, as my study in my apartment (which should give you an idea of how little money *some* pathologists make). There was a large lamp, turned on, illuminating the passage.

But what caught everyone's eye were the footprints—bloody footprints, to be more precise. They led all the way down the passage in both directions: some facing away from us and some leading towards the room.

What struck even me, and I'm no footprint expert, is that there were *two* sets of footprints. One average-sized and the other somewhat larger. I glanced at the feet around me to get a sense of the sizes of the feet around me. I looked at Perkins's feet—small. The largest pair of feet in the room belonged to Helen Freud! I was surprised, but then there was no reason why Helen Freud couldn't have large feet. Large feet aren't something you can plan, like how much ketchup to put on your burger. You just get them, like scabies and dust-mite allergies. And so, clearly, when Nature had rolled out her dice, Helen won the humongous feet lottery.

The footprint experts were at these bloody footprints like a bunch of savage bloodhounds. There was one senior guy and one who appeared more junior, with a large camera, being instructed on how to take the photographs.

Freud requested—no, commanded—Perkins to bring her one of Zimaresh's shoes. While he went to do so, we walked down the passage, taking care to avoid the bloody footprints. That's one of the problems with these crime scenes: you've got to be super careful not to tamper with or destroy the evidence. And so there we were, like cautious cats, tiptoeing and rubbing against the walls down the pathway.

We soon came into a room. This was the barest possible room, with few trappings or decorations, almost identical to some of the rooms I'd lived in as a poor medical student. There was a long, large table in the center. The table was covered with—you guessed it, clotted blood. (This should have given me an idea about the problem with the blood in the study, but it didn't—I would connect the dots just a bit later.)

Somebody had made some effort to scrub off some of the blood, but there was still enough for us to make some kind of determination.

"Simon," I said, "Can you take a sample of this?"

Simon argued his point as follows:

"But I've already taken some from the study—the quality of the one I've taken is better because it's still liquid in the room but clotted here."

"Something doesn't seem right to me. Take it, and we'll run this blood as well as the blood in the room."

For those of you puzzled by the terminology, "running the blood" simply refers to running lab tests on the blood.

Simon began his task, trying to gently get some of the clotted blood from the table and some from the floor.

Meanwhile, Perkins stood in front of us, carrying a pair of shiny black shoes in a glinting, gleaming silver tray.

14

"The size of these shoes is about the same as the smaller footprints," said Mason, one of the criminal investigators. "They're not the same—identical—shoes that produced the footprints though—I'll need to do a more thorough evaluation—but I can tell you straight away that although they don't match the prints exactly, they're approximately the same size, which is not saying much."

Freud didn't seem to pay any attention to Mason.

"Perkins," she bellowed, "Does this room lead anywhere outside?"

"As madam can see," she said, "There are no doors or windows in this room."

"Yes, Madam can see that there are no doors or windows. But your boss was a very—unusual—man. There are no secret tunnels or passages, are there?"

"Only the passage you came down yourself. I refer to the passage from the study to this room. Madam can check and make sure for herself, but as far as I'm aware, there is no way out of this room other than the one leading into the study."

"Oh, Madam can check, can she? Well, madam *will* check," she said humorlessly, without much conviction. Zimaresh had been correct in his letter. Perkins was a very well-informed man—every word that came out of his mouth sounded well-informed, complete with a seal of authority. If Perkins said that there was no way out of this room, then we could be sure that there was no way out of this room, and we could be sure we wouldn't find out. Because Perkins said so. But Freud had to make sure, of course. Just like she had to send her boys down through the trees and into the underground tunnel running beneath the study to make sure that the murderer wasn't hiding in there. Nobody had really expected that the killer was lurking there, for the police to come and catch him, but, as I said, these are the kinds of things one has to check and be certain about.

"The footprints are the last straw!" Freud said whimsically. "So now we have two sets of footprints, which means that we have *two* killers. This means we're looking for not one vanishing killer but *two* killers who disappeared from a locked room they couldn't have disappeared from, carrying a head with them. And a weapon, too, like an axe or something. It's just impossible!" She changed the subject, "So Zimaresh was murdered on this table. He could hardly have walked down the path after he'd had his head cut off. But, surprise, surprise, his shoe size matches the size of the smaller footprints. Maybe you're right, Dr. Chaplin, and Zimaresh is the killer, and some other poor fellow is sitting in the room minus a head. But of course, many people share shoe sizes, and this killer could be a similar size as Mr. Zimaresh."

There was a respectful cough at this point, and there was Perkins, whom Freud had forgotten to dismiss after he'd brought the shoes.

"Yes, Perkins, I presume you wish to say something."

"Madam is practically a psychic," said Perkins with a tiny flourish. "I can attest to the fact that the shoes worn by Mr. Zimaresh are indeed those belonging to Mr. Zimaresh. I mean to say that the shoes worn by the deceased individual in the study are unquestionably those that were owned by Mr. Zimaresh. I have observed them from a distance—one can't venture too close because of the police. I mean, these are your rules, but those are his shoes: he acquired them from Monsieur Gramadine in Belgium—a very fine, though comparatively unknown crafter of exquisite shoes, if I may add. If you evaluate the shoes worn by the dead man, you will notice Mr. Zimaresh's name monogrammed in gold on the inside."

"Thank you, Perkins." Freud sounded genuinely grateful. "A little more evidence that the dead man is Zimaresh."

"I hate to disappoint you, Helen," I said, "But a shoe is hardly an identifying characteristic. For example, the shoes I'm wearing now belong to my sister. And I can swear to you that I'm not my sister."

Freud looked at me irritably.

"I said a little more evidence. Not conclusive evidence. I am well aware that shoes don't make the man." She paused before continuing, "You're the pathologist, you tell us who this dead guy is. I'll just stick to the other facts."

Meanwhile, someone—one of the officers—approached Freud, holding something in his gloved hands. It was a white container, wider in the middle and tapering towards both ends. One of the ends was open, and there was a spout coming off from the side. The thing was made of plastic; imagine an open-topped kettle that is wider in the middle, and you will know what this peculiar object looked like. I certainly had never seen anything like it in my life.

"You'd better take a look inside," said Mason to me, with a look of great significance in his eyes.

Inside was a small amount of bright red—blood. Not clotted blood, but liquid. I took the container from his hand and sloshed the blood about. And then, of course, I understood what was wrong with the blood in the study. It should've been sort of obvious, but this pot made it crystal clear in my mind.

But I think Freud was more interested in the superficial aspects of this pot or whatever it was.

"What is that thing?"

"That, madam, is what the natives refer to as a *lota*. That's L-O-T-A," Perkins said, spelling it out, ready with the information.

"*Lota?* What natives?"

"Mr. Zimaresh acquired this structure from India. He had gone there researching one of his novels, I believe, *Murder in a Harem*, no pardon me, it was *The Biryani Murders*, the *biryani* being a popular dish, probably

Afghan in origin, consisting of colored rice, spices, raisins, and succulent meat, chicken, beef or lamb—"

Freud seemed ready to erupt with impatience. She interrupted him: "Okay, great. What do you do with this thing? You can't cook tea in it or something. It's plastic."

Perkins let out a soft chuckle. "Forgive me, madam, but I found that a bit amusing, as you will too once you discover the use to which the lota is put. No, the Indians and Pakistanis certainly don't cook tea in the *lota*. They use it for a far more basic purpose. Following the act of excretion, they use the *lota*, filled with water, to bathe and cleanse the anatomic structures that have become soiled by the aforementioned excretory activities."

"You mean after crapping, they rinse their ass with water from this thing?" Freud asked indelicately.

"Precisely. Madam has a gift for being to the point. The artistically curved spout, you will observe, allows for precisely directing the efflux of water upon—as you refer to it—the 'ass' and neighboring locales. I've been told that they make use of one hand in a rubbing, rotary motion while holding the *lota* in the other hand and pouring water down from it. The net effect of these maneuvers is to achieve a far greater degree of cleanliness than may be achieved by mere toilet paper."

"Oh, you know this from experience," asked Freud testily.

"Alas, madam, I never quite got the hang of it. It is easier said than done. It requires great dexterity, and the rubbing motion deep down there is more complicated than I make it sound. Apparently, the people in the Indian subcontinent learn to use this device from early childhood and have, therefore, a strong foundation for achieving excellence in the use of the *lota*."

Perkins' words sparked a train of recollections inside my head. Yes, I had seen a *lota* before, and not just once but many times. In toilets in Indian and Pakistani restaurants, of course. Until now, I had merely regarded them with indifference, unclear as to their actual purpose. Now it suddenly became clear why the things were sometimes filled with water, sometimes empty. I started viewing my Pakistani and Indian friends in a new light. They did something I did not do. If you got past the disgust factor of cleaning your dirty behind with your bare hand, I think the end result would be cleaner, no?

But this was no time to compare cultural differences in bathroom habits. There was the important clue of the blood. I had essential information to share. All because of an all-important *lota* with sloshing blood inside it.

"This blood," I said quietly (but dramatically; once in a while, I too feel the need to be a little dramatic, to bask in the admiration of attentive, appreciative looks), "is not clotting, but all the other blood in this room is clotted. The blood in the study is also kind of liquid-y. But not the blood around the neck of the victim, which is clotted, as is the blood on his shirt and tux. So we have some blood that is clotted and some blood that is not clotted. That is strange. Also, if he was killed in this room, why is there so much blood in the study? We would've expected most of the blood to be in *this* room, and we do have a lot of blood, *but it is clotted except for the blood in this lota.* Confusing, yes?"

"Why would the blood not clot?"

"They could've used some chemical that prevents clotting. An anticoagulant, like the ones they use in blood banks all the time—you know, to give transfusions. You can't give clotted blood to patients—it kind of defeats the purpose. Hence, the anticoagulant, a chemical that prevents clotting. Obviously, the killer obtained some anticoagulant—"

"Killer*s*," corrected Freud, "And where do you get this anticoagulant from? The neighborhood pharmacy?"

"Well, I don't know," I confessed. The last time I purchased some anticoagulant was…well, never…I mean, when was the last time *you* popped into the pharmacy to buy an anticoagulant for a bunch of blood?

But I had a thought.

"They need not have bought any anticoagulant. I mean, the easiest thing would've been to somehow get into a blood bank and steal some blood. They're kept in these plastic bags—half a liter or so of blood in a bag. They could've stolen several bags, emptied them into this *lota* thing, and soaked the place with it."

Freud summed it up:

"So these killers, they kill Mr. Zimaresh in this room, move his corpse to his study, then pour some *other* blood that they stole from a blood bank, use the announcement system to let people know that he's been murdered, wait for us to come, and then somehow magically disappear with the head. Impossible!"

Something struck me.

"The voice that was heard, was it definitely Zimaresh's?"

Perkins answered me, "Without a doubt, madam."

I said: "So they must have taped Zimaresh calling for help, played the tape over the announcement system, and then took the tape with them as well. Or maybe they got Zimaresh to make the announcement, brought him to this room, got him to lie down here on this table, cut off his head, moved his body to the study, and then, along with head and weapon, they—as you said—magically disappeared. As easy as one-two-three…unless that's not the way it happened at all."

15

In a typical mystery story, the mystery writer wants you to believe and think in a certain way—a way that is obviously wrong. She—or he—leads you down the wrong track. You jump to the wrong conclusions. Then, in the end, the writer springs her trap on you, and you shake your head and wonder, now why did I let myself be fooled?

Later that night, shortly before I tried to catch a few hours of sleep, I thought about mystery writers and the kinds of lies they tell you. I felt this was an important point and one that was being ignored by Helen Freud. I jotted down some notes. See if you agree with my point of view:

Fact: Zimaresh appears to have committed suicide with the help of someone, in a crime that is, for all practical purposes, impossible.

Fact: Zimaresh has left a bunch of clues to help us figure out how this supposedly impossible happening happened.

Fact: Zimaresh is (or was) a mystery writer.

So, putting all these facts together, I could only come up with the following conclusion, which I wrote down as follows:

*Zimaresh, a mystery writer, for reasons that we don't know, is making donkeys out of the whole bunch of us. He's not the dead man, some other guy is. Which means that we are dealing with a cold-blooded murder—make that an **impossible** cold-blooded murder, and the murderer has to be Zimaresh.*

Well, that's how I reasoned. But then, my bed began to have an effect on me, and I yawned, and before I knew it, I was elsewhere, far away from Zimaresh and all the other worries of the world.

In no time at all, after a brief sleep, the next day yawned upon me. Do you know what I mean? You know how you have some days that just sort of eat you up, consume you, and leave you feeling totally spent? Well, this was one such day. A big giant yawn of a day, and I got sucked into it.

When I woke up from a nearly dreamless sleep, I did not know what terrors lay before me. I'm not exaggerating. When I say "terrors," I mean it quite literally. Like the terror you feel when you've barely escaped death—completely by chance, but that it could happen again.

It began with the letter. Left on my desk.

I saw it immediately. The same faint yellow tinge to it, like the envelope I had seen the day before. The same words, written the same way.

FOR IMOGENE CHAPLIN

I felt a sick feeling. As far as I was concerned, Zimaresh was a sicko who'd gone off the deep end. I suppose if I were far removed from the whole business, I might feel sorrow and compassion for the poor guy. But I was not far removed from this business; I was inside the damn business. In my mind, Zimaresh was guilty. Probably, when mystery writers go mad, this is what happens to them. They stage an impossible murder. But when you've staged one impossible murder, what's to stop you from staging two? Or three?

I didn't like the fact that this nutcase was leaving letters for *me* all over the place. When would he stop leaving letters and start leaving something else, like, say, a knife in my back? I felt a tingle in my back at this thought, right between the shoulder blades, a perfect spot to slide a stiletto in, tearing lung and heart—and with it, giving wings to my earthly life.

But how'd he gotten past the front desk in the first place? The medical examiner's office is secured at the front window. There's a bolted door that can be opened from the inside by the person sitting at the front window. This person, Lucius Spriggs, happened to be a weak-looking guy with very powerful lungs. He sang in his church choir and, by all accounts, was a powerful tenor who could, when he had to, sound almost like a wailing soprano. None of this was put to good use by him.

Bright and early in the morning, a woman—a very large woman, a blonde with dark glasses—walked up to the front window. She presented a note to Mr. Spriggs, a simple one that said, "I'VE GOT A GUN. I WILL USE IT ON YOUR CHEST. OPEN THE DOOR." To the point, it got the message across. Mr. Spriggs got the message. He obliged rapidly, clearly being as fond of his earthly life as I am. The next thing that happened was that the woman whacked him on the nose with a heavy punch, knocking him out flat, not giving him a chance to scream or sing out a warning. Then, this woman must have chloroformed him—rendering him unconscious. If you're wondering where everybody else was—well, there was nobody else there, right there in the front window area—there are never too many people there, and besides, it was very early in the morning. There were only a few lab technicians (but they were in the lab), and, as I discovered later on, Dr. Felicity Moon, my senior colleague, had come in earlier, a little before Spriggs.

As I walked in (later than usual), the police officers had just about dissipated. I got the scoop from my secretary. My secretary—actually, she is not just my secretary, she is everybody's secretary—appears what technically can be described as a sweet old (or oldish) lady with a grandmotherly fragrance about her. Rebecca Winslet (for such is her name) enacted the episode with great drama. There was Lucius Spriggs, defenseless choir singer and receptionist, who wisely made no attempt to resist the large woman with "a lot of balls" (Rebecca's words, not mine; like many grandmothers who've seen a lot of the world, she doesn't shrink from using strong words when the situation demands it); this villainous lady then overpowered poor Spriggs ("even a small lady without any balls could've overpowered Spriggs, have you seen how tiny he is?"—once again, I'm quoting Rebecca).

I asked: "Why did this woman do this? Why attack poor Spriggs? It's not like we've got any treasures hidden in the medical examiner's office."

Rebecca had a theory. "It's all the drugs they have in the chemical lab." She was referring to the section of the lab devoted to chemicals recovered from criminals, including large quantities of narcotics, hallucinogens, and so on.

"But was that place broken into?"

"Amelia and Dick were in there at the time, but they didn't see this woman trying to break in."

I gently tried to point out the problem with her hypothesis: "But that means she wasn't trying to get to the drugs."

"Maybe she saw Amelia and Dick in there and changed her mind."

"She was prepared to use a gun on Spriggs, whose nose she's almost broken. Why would she suddenly change her mind? My guess is that this woman came in for some other reason."

"Well, I don't know what then?" Rebecca said thoughtfully.

Neither did the police, it seemed, as Rebecca pointed out. As far as they could tell, this woman had forced herself into the premises, done something, and then left before Spriggs was found on his back in the front office by one of the investigators who came to drop in some evidence.

I didn't connect this event with the bizarre murder of the night before. But I did so as soon as I discovered the envelope in my office. The envelope with the words **FOR IMOGENE CHAPLIN**. Then I knew why the large woman (*who probably had proportionately large feet*) had felt the need to punch Spriggs in the nose and drug him. She had to make a delivery.

A delivery.

For me.

A delivery from one of killers…

16

I thought about opening the letter but then decided against it. This was evidence, and I would wait till Helen Freud got here (she was on her way).

I sat in my chair to unwind. The body of Zimaresh, or whoever the dead guy was, sat in the cooler. I wasn't ready to attack that project yet.

I rang Felicity Moon. She wasn't in her office. I left her a message, asking her to call me back. With Spence out of town, I needed to discuss the case with a senior person—someone who breathed and drank forensic pathology. Felicity Moon, I'd known her only briefly, was an intense and well-known expert in the field.

I drummed my fingers on the desk. My desk is very wide. My chair, a swiveling kind with wheels, can go in almost all the way into the desk and still leave room beneath it for me to stretch my legs. Stretching my legs seemed to be a nice idea, and so I tried it. But I failed because my shoe bumped into something. And then I felt something warm trickling down my foot.

Needless to say, I jumped as if I'd accidentally found a cockroach crawling down my back.

I think I must have screamed. In fact, I'm almost sure I screamed, even though I don't remember exactly. But in a few moments, there were suddenly a bunch of people in my office. I mean Rebecca, a couple of investigators, and I don't remember who else.

My next remark was unmemorable. I think I said something like, "Um-ah-er-my desk," and jabbed repeatedly in the direction of my desk while at the same time sprinting away from it.

I'm embarrassed to admit that I'd lost my head a bit. I'd like to be able to say I was cool and controlled and kept my wits about me, but I didn't. I just panicked. First, the letter. Now, something below my desk.

I looked at my foot and my shoe—the one I'd poked into this something—whatever it was.

Blood.

A sickening feeling crept over my body.

"Not another body!" I whispered, knowing full well that it was precisely a body and nothing but a body, a human person's body, that lay beneath my desk.

We were soon all peeking below the desk.

The scent of a sweet perfume, tinged with the familiar, metallic odor of blood, assailed my nostrils. And curled below my desk, even though I couldn't see her that well, was Dr. Felicity Moon. I mean, *the body* of Dr. Felicity Moon, sadly, without any signs of life.

17

My office officially became a crime scene. This meant that everything in it was now potentially evidence, including my purse, my scrubs, a half-eaten sandwich from the day before, and an opened box of organic chips. Helen Freud was soon all over my office (and all over poor Felicity) with her crew (fewer policemen than the night before—far fewer). The place was one big mess of activity, with people taking pictures, collecting evidence in plastic bags, bending over this or that. Felicity's outlines were chalked, with considerable difficulty, on the undersurface of my desk. The guy who did the chalking had to be something of a contortionist.

A dark stain of blood had seeped from her body out upon the carpeted floor of my office.

Felicity herself was moved out in a rather undignified way. She'd been a charming woman in life. But when you've been bunched up, dead, beneath a desk, then it is a tussle to move you out and carry you away. Not even the most elegant human being can continue to remain elegant after she's been killed and then carried by plumpish cops. That's just the way life is—I mean to say, that's the way death is. Nothing stays the same forever.

Felicity was still warm when I touched her forehead. I had to. Being the only pathologist on the scene and officially the only person acting in the capacity of a medical examiner, I did what I had to, but not without resistance.

"Where the hell is Spence?" I snapped at Rebecca.

"In Denmark, dear," she answered me, not in the least put out by my tone. She rubbed my arm kindly as if anticipating my need to be humored and coddled at this difficult time.

"Denmark—yes—" I said, remembering something Simon had mentioned to me the previous night. "Oh wait a minute, wasn't it Denver?"

"It was Den-something," said Rebecca, sounding a bit distant and confused. "But he comes back this afternoon—or is it tomorrow afternoon?"

Meanwhile, I felt a tap on my shoulder.

It was Helen Freud.

She was holding the letter in her hand.

Dear Imogene (the new letter said),

I envy you your life. Life gives you the opportunity to solve the little problem I have set for you. To go over some important points:

I am, as you have no doubt figured out by now, quite dead: very few people survive the process of decapitation!

Is there a part of you that wonders that perhaps I am not really dead? I suspect that you might have, like so many women of my acquaintance, a suspicious nature. Well, let me state quite clearly that I really am dead. This is the promise of a dead man to you. In case you don't believe me, why not try to go about identifying my body? That should tell you something.

Now let me introduce you to another problem. (You, because you are not an expert forensic pathologist at this point, need my help in getting the job done—and so I am spending considerable time and energy going over every little detail that I possibly can.) Basically, the lack of my head should make it difficult for you. Difficult, yes, but not impossible. You can do DNA analysis from my corpse—but then you would need a DNA sample that you know belongs to me to compare with. Where will you find such a sample? Does such a sample exist? I'm not about to tell you, but it wouldn't hurt to get a DNA analysis done on my body.

I will tell you a simpler method of identifying my body. You can use any distinguishing features on the remainder of my anatomy. But how will you do that? You could try Perkins—but he has seen me naked only infrequently. A man is supposed to have no secrets from his valet, but I always felt squeamish about undressing in front of a man, any man, no matter how good a valet he is. But women! Ah, this body of mine, when it lived and breathed and walked and talked, was made for women. A machine built for pleasure—now sadly no longer! Ah, such is life. Good or bad, one has to take it and make the best of a terrible job.

*So here is my letter to help you out. Read over the last paragraph to see the valuable clue I have left for you. And by the way, did you ever find the clue I mentioned in my previous letter? I refer to the following one: <u>Number six: For you to figure out</u>. If you haven't already, and I pity your brain if you haven't, please re-read the **first** paragraph of my **first** letter to you. Do you remember how it goes? I am copying it here for your convenience:*

<u>*I hope you don't mind me calling you by your first name. After all, I am writing this, one of the very last things I will ever write, to you, and in the last few weeks, I feel that I've come to know you rather well. It's a pity we never had a chance to be intimate, though I assure you that you would have found an experience with me to be quite phenomenal and exhilarating. You may care to check out testimonials in that regard, if you like. In the top left-hand drawer, you will find a little green book (I find the convention of a little black book quite tiresome, don't you agree?). In this book, you will find the names of all my—I hate to use the word—conquests, but I assure you all these conquests of mine yielded to me not only willingly but enthusiastically.*</u>

*Got it now? Do the words **little green book** suggest anything to you? Only the sixth clue…*

Yours in spirit,

George Zimaresh

P.S. There is another clue you could pass on to the police (what can we do about the police? They are the ones who always get it wrong—at least in my books. But don't worry, I have faith in you). Here's the clue. It's a name. Marion Best.

18

P.S. There is another clue you could pass on to the police (what can we do about the police? They are the ones who always get it wrong—at least in my books. But don't worry, I have faith in you). Here's the clue. It's a name. Marion Best.

"Marion Best. That name sounds familiar," said Freud. "We'll have to check him out."

Then, after a pause, she said: "Why does he keep writing to you? Does he know you? Yes, yes, I know he doesn't, but it's driving me crazy why he keeps sending *you* letters." It was driving me crazy, too. She then snorted disapprovingly, as if to say that she would've preferred Zimaresh to have sent the letters to her instead of to me. I've always found snorting to be a fascinating process. I am a non-snorter. I find the action, I mean snorting, to be a difficult one. You have to blow air through your nose and make a sound. Difficult, if not impossible, for me. Also, isn't there a small chance that you could snort a little too vigorously and end up with— you know—snot all over the place? Snort does not automatically equal snot, but it might if you are a clumsy operator.

I was momentarily distracted by Freud's impressive snort, but almost instantaneously, I marshaled my thoughts to the most important subject at hand. Felicity Moon was dead. And the murderer had left a letter on my desk.

A horrible thought passed though my head: *Was I the intended victim?*

I pitied poor Felicity. But you know, at least I was still alive for the time being. How long would my good luck last?

There is nothing as terrible as wondering whether you are breathing on borrowed time (which all of us *are*, every moment of our lives, but most of us don't usually think of it this way). It's like being in an unusual prison—with knives falling out of the sky. They may miss you now and then, but you know it's only a matter of time before a knife pierces a vital part of your anatomy.

I must have looked worried. For Freud seemed to have read my thoughts.

"Cheer up," she said. "I don't think this killer was trying to kill you."

I wanted to believe her. "Why?"

"Read the letter. This psycho wants you to live. He wants to help you solve this mystery. Or at least that's what he claims. He's leaving letters for you all over the place. Does this mean he wants to kill you?"

"Maybe not now. How about later?"

"When *later* comes, we'll think about *later*," Freud said philosophically.

"Oh, thanks, that cheers me up tremendously." I was a bit irritated. People have every right to be philosophical—as long as it is not about *my* impending death. I'm not unusual in this respect. Like most people, I find it easier to rationalize and philosophize about other people's deaths. When the subject becomes personal, i.e., my own death, I become far less detached.

"So now you agree that this bozo is alive and nuts."

"You mean Zimaresh?"

"Who else?"

"It's a possibility, of course—but the man swears he's dead in this letter," said Freud.

"Oh yes, of course, and there's no chance he might be lying, right?" I said sarcastically.

"It's up to you," said Freud tersely. "Your job. Identify the body. By the way, I've got the little green book here."

But I had my hands full at the moment. The late Dr. Felicity Moon was waiting for me in the autopsy room.

19

Somebody had smashed a heavy object into her head—with enough force to crack her skull. Congealed blood pasted her golden hair, covered the back of her neck, and ran all over her pretty white blouse. But, oddly, this killer had also driven a knife through her chest.

"Odd," I said to Freud, who stood silently chewing on a mint.

"What's odd?"

"She had a gun—this big blonde that threatened Spriggs with it."

"Yes," said Freud.

"So why not use the gun? Why smash her head and then kill her with a knife? Was she carrying a knife with her as well?"

"A gun is noisy. Maybe she didn't want to attract any more attention."

"But why kill Felicity?"

"She was in your office."

"I see." I suppose it was possible. "You mean our female killer walks into my office to drop off this letter for me, sees Felicity, is surprised, picks up something heavy, and kills her. Then, just to make sure, she uses a knife on her. But why go through all this trouble? She could've waited a little bit for Felicity to leave my office."

"Maybe Felicity saw her?"

"Felicity was attacked on the *back* of her head. She's unlikely to have turned her back to the killer unless she knew him. No, the thing doesn't make sense. It's almost as if Felicity saw this woman coming out of my office, and the woman saw her; Felicity went inside my office, the killer goes back, picks up something heavy, and smashes it on the back of her head. Then knifes her. But even that is unlikely."

"Why?" asked Freud.

"Think about it. This big blonde is not afraid to be seen. She threatens Spriggs, knocks him out, but doesn't kill him—why? *Because she's not afraid of being recognized.*"

Freud broke in quickly, "So, maybe she was disguised in some way, and Dr. Moon recognized her. And the killer couldn't take a chance."

The little green book was both little and green. It was divided into sections labeled with alphabets from A to Z. Very few people I know have many entries for Z. But he did. His daughter, Amelia Zimaresh, was listed in the Z's. She lived in the West University neighborhood of Houston. There was also a Zenobia Zimaresh, who turned out to be his ex-wife (she decided not to change her name). There were, in fact, eighteen Zimareshes listed, including an elderly aunt (in Alaska, living with his older brother, Merrick Zimaresh). There were other Z's as well in this list, including a Zeldon and a Zanthoper, both women. Lydia Zanthoper and Mariette Zeldon. Both were listed simply as "LOVER."

This is what I was looking for, and so Zimaresh made my task much easier.

A lover, even an ex-lover, knows things about your anatomy that other acquaintances and friends don't. Maybe you have a mole or cyst in an embarrassing spot—or a scar somewhere. This is what I needed. Something obvious. I needed a lover to walk into the autopsy suite and tell me what I already knew: that the headless corpse was not Zimaresh.

All in all, there were more than a hundred women who were all listed as lovers. A hundred-and-twenty-two, to be precise. Clearly, Zimaresh, who had written close to fifty books, had time for much else.

I was dazed by this barrage of lover after lover after lover. I obviously couldn't have a hundred and twenty-two lovers trampling in and out of the autopsy suite.

Could there be an easier way?

Zimaresh had a grading system for his lovers. Many—the majority—had a single star beside their name. Others had two, fewer still had three, only ten or so four star-holders and an exclusive five-star lover: a Magdalene Fitzpatrick, who lived not very far away, also in the River Oaks region.

A man need have no secrets from his little green book, so I could not blame Zimaresh for rating his lovers. It must get complicated to keep things straight on the love-angle when you have a hundred and twenty-two prospects to choose from. Also, being a writer, and a famous one at that, I had no doubt that the man must have wanted to write an autobiography. Having your lovers rated in a simple way is a major asset when it comes to writing your biography. Can you imagine how difficult it is, when you're beginning to go senile, to ask yourself something like: now let me see, was Lydia Zanthoper a four or a one? (She was a three, in case you're wondering.)

20

I began with Magdalene Fitzpatrick, Zimaresh's five-star lover.

I don't know what I was expecting from a "five-star" kind of woman, but Magdalene Fitzpatrick wasn't anywhere close to it. She was a woman in her early forties, with practically no curvature to her silhouette. When I try to think like a man, I imagine that most men would prefer some body in a woman, some curves. A woman may be thin like some supermodels, but even these supermodels have shape and curvature. Not Magdalene Fitzpatrick. She was thin, stick-like, and quite devoid of anything even remotely resembling roundness. Her face was long and angular. But appealing—she had large, I suppose soulful, eyes and a largish mouth, with pouty lips. This was because of her teeth, which jutted out somewhat and for which she used braces.

There was something indefinably attractive about her. And her voice. Sensuous and husky. She had a child-like gaze. That's what she was, very much like a kid. She was a strange choice for a top-rated lover. However, Zimaresh was an odd fellow, and he could hardly be expected to have a normal choice in women. But what did it matter? Magdalene F. had five stars, and I needed her for a single purpose: identification.

She looked white and ill at ease. Naturally, the autopsy suite has an artificial, sickeningly sweet smell about it. The alternative is to have a very real make-you-throw-up kind of aroma. In the center of this grey and well-lighted room lay the body of a man without a head. Naked. He had to be. After all, you can't ask someone to examine someone else's anatomy without exposing it—the anatomy, I mean. And so far, nobody has found a genteel, discreet way of making naked look less naked, if you know what I mean. (All I had done was to cover the top of his body, from the shoulders up, so that one couldn't tell that the head was missing (I didn't want lovers and ex-lovers getting too much of a shock), and out of respect for the dead, a green towel was placed upon the groin area, as is typical in these cases. The rest of the pale white body was visible.)

"Oh no!" she gasped. "This is terrible, terrible! Just terrible!"

She seemed genuinely upset.

"I loved him," she said, taking a deep breath and then quickly added, "I mean, like a brother!"

"Brother?" This was an unexpected remark. I wasn't looking for a sister. "But I thought you were—"

"Lovers? Yes," she said, suddenly very composed. "We *used* to be lovers, and Roger loved him too."

"Roger?"

"My ex-husband. Also my future husband, since we've decided to put the past behind us and get back together. He was very confused. You see, George was a charismatic person. Very few people could resist him. Roger thought he was in love with him, but that's nonsense. Roger wasn't in love with him. Not unless he'd turned gay for the sake of one person. And people don't do that, do they? You're a doctor, you know."

Of course, I knew nothing of the sort. But I nodded thoughtfully, appearing, I hope, wise and understanding.

"It was a crazy time. I was in love with George, and Roger and I were married, and both of us wanted to sleep with George. It drove me mad. I threw Roger out of the house. Asked for a divorce. I mean, enough's enough."

I thought it best to interrupt this flow.

"So you think you can identify the body as that of Mr. Zimaresh's?"

"Oh, will I have to look at this body?"

"I'm afraid there's no other way for you to tell short of actually looking at him."

"But I can't bear it!"

"It won't take long! It could be someone else."

"Someone else! But that's preposterous!"

"Why so preposterous?"

"I mean, it was him in his study. Dead. Right? He told me he was going to die."

"He did. When?"

"Three months ago. He'd been to the doctor."

I was confused. "He told you three months ago that he'd die last night."

Magdalene sighed, "No, of course he didn't. But he was going to die. He was very ill."

"Very ill?"

"Cancer."

"Cancer?"

"Terrible, right?"

"Very. What kind of cancer?"

"I don't know. But very bad. Three months, or six months, or some horribly short time. That's what he told me. He told me he wasn't going to just die, just like that. He told me he was going to die in an amazing way."

"This is amazing, all right," I muttered.

"Oh, I absolutely agree with you!" she said, suddenly brightening up. "It's all over the news—you know, TV and the papers. How do you think he did it? They said it was an impossible murder."

"It's impossible, yes. Nobody quite understands how it was done."

"That's the way George was! So inventive and brilliant. If only he were alive to hear you. It's horrible when people have to die, isn't it?" she asked childishly.

What a strange mixture of adult and child!

I half-wondered if I ought to take her hand and lead her to the corpse. I had no idea how she would react. Would she be able to take it?

"If you will come closer to him," I suggested.

"He's without his head—it's true what they say about his head, isn't it?"

"Yes, I'm afraid so. This is why I need you to take a look at him. Maybe there's something else?"

"Oh, but, but, his most impressive part—" she stopped. "It's very embarrassing—how to say it?"

"Oh, please don't be shy. Please. It's very necessary."

"I mean, it's the—er—you know—I mean, he was very *well-endowed*."

I shook my head. No matter how well-endowed a man might have been in life, private parts are not a reliable way of identifying the dead. Not unless there's an injury or a birthmark or some such identifying feature—

But I didn't want to discourage her. She was trying, after all, to help.

I removed the green towel covering his crotch. Magdalene gave a gasp. "That's not him!"

"How can you be so sure?" This was Freud, who had until now managed to stay quiet in the background. But she was there, watching Magdalene very carefully. I had caught Freud's eye a couple of times, looking puzzled, amused, and even suspicious.

"Yes, Ms. Fitzpatrick, how can you be certain?" I asked her as well.

"Like I said, George was very, extraordinary. It was much, much fuller, you know. That's not his you-know-what."

"But Ms. Fitzpatrick, he's dead. Things change after death. The organ you refer to is a changeable one, as I don't have to explain to you. In the heat of the moment, I have no doubt that he, or it, felt—felt quite different. You can't compare the present shriveled state of the organ with the splendid way it may have been in life. It's not a reliable indicator. I can tell you quite authoritatively that this is not one of the acceptable ways of identifying a dead man. Can't you think of something else? Like a birthmark or something?"

She took a moment, surveying the body as she reflected. Then she shook her head.

"It's not him," she said.

"Why?" I asked.

"He had a birthmark on his knee. It was a pretty big, black thing, a mole, with a bunch of hairs coming out of it. This man has no such thing on his knee."

"Which knee?"

"The left."

The left knee of this individual was unblemished. I ran my finger over it. Smooth. It is possible he could've had it removed, but would it have been so smooth? I imagine a good plastic surgeon could have removed the mole and not left a mark.

"Maybe he had it removed…"

"I don't think so. He was very proud of it. He used to joke about it: My lucky birthmark, he used to say. He said people could spot him from a distance just by looking at his knee."

"But he could've changed his mind."

She looked at me with exasperation as if I were an idiot child, being more idiotic than usual.

"I saw it."

"When?"

"Yesterday, before the party. He was wearing shorts. I saw his knee, and he still had it."

"You were at his house *before* the party?" Freud stirred.

"Yes—some hours before the party. I got him a CD. I thought he might want to play it at the party."

"How did he look?"

"Busy. He had a couple of visitors, he said, and so he couldn't stop and chat. I just gave him the CD and left."

"And you were able to see his knee."

"Well, I don't specifically remember looking at his knee."

Freud interrupted, "So you didn't see his knee yesterday."

"No, I didn't stare at his knee," she replied indignantly. "There was no reason to ogle at his knee."

"So, for all you know, it's possible that he didn't have the mole on his knee yesterday? Because you didn't actually look at his knee, you know; you had no need to."

"Yes, I didn't. I admit that. But I tell you, if it had not been there, I would've noticed it, right? You couldn't miss it. It was as broad as a—as a—well, as a couple of silver dollars. That's not him. That's not George. But that—what does that mean?"

"But Ms. Fitzpatrick, you didn't actually focus on the knee. So, how can you be sure? When was the last time you took a really good look at his knee?"

"I can't remember," she said with irritation. "I don't go about looking at people's knees. I know that mole of his catches—caught—my eye when we were together, but that was a while back."

"OK. Thanks. Now, one more question. I have to ask you about the visitors—the ones you mentioned, the ones before the party," said Freud.

"But I can't tell you anything about them. George didn't tell me who they were. I never saw them." She appeared to think a little, and then she asked me,

"But can I ask a question first?"

"Go ahead," I said.

"I don't mean to pry or anything, but how come *you* don't remember the mole?" It took me a second to realize that she was asking me.

"How can *I* remember the mole?" I raised my voice a little but softened my voice immediately. "I've never seen George Zimaresh's knee."

"Oh, you haven't. But that's—but that's strange…"

"Why so strange?" Really, the woman was maddeningly insane. I could easily imagine lunatic asylums competing for her business.

"It's like in the news—they said so on TV."

"They said on TV that I'd seen Mr. Zimaresh's knee!"

"No, they didn't say that. They said nothing about his knee or you seeing it. Just that, just that, well, that you may have been, you know—"

"No, I don't know!" I was losing my patience.

"They think that the two of you may have been lovers. You and Zimaresh. I don't believe everything in the media—I'm just telling you what I heard."

21

Lovers.

So, what else was new? This is exactly the kind of development that one should anticipate in life. Generations of philosophers and wise ones have imparted this wisdom: Expect the unexpected. We know this. It is embedded in our genes, almost. And yet, whenever Fate throws us an unexpected curve ball, we act as if the unexpected is the most unexpected thing that could happen to us.

Yes, life doesn't follow a straight line. You go to the grocery to buy milk but fall in love with another customer/store manager/security guard, etc., forget all about the milk, and come home with a copy of a magazine that teaches you how to please your man—or something like that. You get run over or get mugged, or something that wasn't supposed to happen happens. This kind of thing doesn't happen every day, just now and then, right around the time you were getting comfortable with the idea that life was nice, orderly, and enjoyable. And suddenly, it's no longer so very enjoyable but hellish.

Hellish. That's the word. As I look back upon this hideous episode in my life, I can think of no word that seems to describe it better. Hellish. It is hellish to receive little love notes from a demented killer. It is hellish to find a colleague bludgeoned and then stabbed to death beneath your desk. And it is especially hellish to find that some jerks in the media are telling everybody that you are the lover of a madman.

I glanced outside the office window—which is to say, outside Spence's office window (I had been temporarily relocated). It was a distressing sight. I saw vans with three- and four-letter words, that is to say, cars belonging to news broadcast stations. I saw reporters. Paparazzi. They were standing there, in the awful heat of spring in Houston, with their cameras, hoping I would come out and chitchat with them. One of the guys, a repulsive toad-like individual, was wiping the back of his neck with his hand and then shaking off the sweat. Another, with trendy dark glasses, was draining a water bottle.

Glumly, I turned my head to Helen Freud. In the last fifteen murders, she had barked orders to several of her underlings. Her last command was to check on Marion Best, the clue mentioned in Zimaresh's last letter to me.

"Well, I have to ask; were you and Zimaresh—"

"What do you think?" I snapped.

"I have to ask."

"Then ask. Here's the answer. Before last night, all I knew of him were his books. And they aren't very clever. Silly stuff, with totally improbable murders."

"Like this one," said Freud.

"Yes, like this one. He's orchestrated this thing—as I've been saying right from the start."

"So he really had the mole?"

"We can easily check that. All we need are a few more lovers in the morgue. And Perkins." I stopped. I remembered something from the night before. Perkins, looking surprised or puzzled.

"Do you know what I think? I think Perkins knows something," I said. This thought burst into my head, pushing aside all the irritating ones about what exactly I was going to say to my mother and my aunts (I have more aunts than any human being can reasonably be expected to have). I had no doubt they had seen the news. Rebecca had passed me a message from my mother a little while ago. *Call me as soon as possible. I'm at Aunt Clara's and am very concerned.*

"What's that?" Freud sat up in the chair. She'd been slouching. Spence's office is full of very comfortable chairs.

"Perkins. Last night, it was as if he was startled, as if he'd suddenly noticed something."

Freud was now sitting on the edge of the chair.

"When?"

"When he stepped past the police tape—you see, it struck me. You saw how he is. Like that super-butler Jeeves, like nothing can bother him. He slipped, and his hair became a bit messy, which he smoothed and carried on as if nothing had happened. But then, he saw something—I think. Something in the room, something around him. He was facing us at the time and facing the corpse as well—maybe it was something about the corpse. But he looked, I don't know, perplexed, surprised. Didn't you notice? *You asked him the name of Zimaresh's publisher, and he didn't even answer.* Now, that's not what they teach you in Butler School. Or is it valet school? I think that Perkins is the sort of guy who answers every question put to him as calmly as is humanly possible, *but he didn't then. You had to ask him again.* Don't you remember?"

Freud nodded. "I do remember. But it could've been because of the whole atmosphere. Let's face it, the place looked like hell, with blood everywhere and, let's not forget, one headless corpse. It's enough to even make someone like *me* lose control."

"Yes, but you're not Perkins. He was Mr. Cool. You saw it. Nothing bothered him. But for that one second, when you asked him about the publisher, he wasn't even listening. Why? I tell you, he saw something. Get it out of him, Helen. Can't you take him to the station and question him?"

22

I was getting desperate. You may object that it was too soon to get desperate. But desperation doesn't look at a clock. Objectively, it had been less than a day since I'd gotten mixed up in this affair, but matters had overwhelmed me.

I didn't want to face any reporters. Have you noticed on TV how they come after some poor soul? And no matter what this person says, he always ends up looking like a liar or a fool.

The only alternative was to find a solution to this mystery. Catch Zimaresh, make him come clean, and then everybody would know that I had nothing to do with it. At least that's what I thought, but looking back, I see that this is a very naïve idea. Once you are labeled as a lover, or if sex enters into the equation somehow, you're forever branded. Ten years later, people might still say something like, oh yes, Zimaresh, wasn't he sleeping with that pathologist, what's her name…

Even so, at some primal level, I felt the urge to solve this puzzle with the same kind of intensity (except much stronger) with which you want to solve a crossword puzzle. I was certain that I wasn't really thinking correctly about the case. Zimaresh had left me—I mean us—clues. I had to assume that the clues were meant to mislead us. But, a part of me said that at least some of them were meant to lead us in the right direction. Why? Well, it's very simple. Zimaresh was a mystery writer. Anyone who has read even one mystery in her life knows that mystery writers leave clues that are designed to lead to the solution, but only if they are looked at in a certain way. In other words, if you look at the clue in the wrong way, you will go totally down the wrong track.

Now consider how Zimaresh had set the whole thing up. He had designed the murder and left clues, just like in a mystery novel. It's like he had inserted us, against our will, into a mystery story. And this was why this story was less like real life and more like fiction. Didn't it follow that his clues had to be fair and at least partially truthful? Or else why go through this complicated business?

I made a small start—a tiny start, by jotting down in my notebook the following notes:

Why?

According to Magdalene F., George Zimaresh had cancer and was going to die. Has she been lied to? My opinion: <u>Lie: he wanted to create a plausible explanation for his "suicide."</u>

The dead man is not George Zimaresh. Magdalene says he had a mole on the left knee; she can't swear she saw it recently, however, but says she'd have noticed if it wasn't there, since Zimaresh was wearing shorts yesterday. This corpse does not have a mole on the left knee. There's not even a wound or a scar to show that a mole was removed.

Magdalene F. could be wrong about the mole. <u>Need to get Perkins and other lovers in to identify the body</u>.

Zimaresh is alive and well or alive and sick (maybe he really has cancer; maybe cancer has driven him mad, and this murder is his way of breaking down. <u>Don't know</u>. Too soon to say.) <u>Need to check with his doctor if he really has cancer. Freud's onto it</u>.

Zimaresh has a motive. Unless he's gone crazy. But the impossible murder, the clues, etc., reveal a lot of planning, which means intelligence. Of course, he could be very clever and very nuts at the same time, but I think he has to have a motive.

Therefore, I need to understand the man. What makes a man do something like this?

<u>Possible motives</u>: Clueless about this. Need to talk to Perkins (he knows something, I'm sure), his daughter, his ex-wife, whoever else knows him well.

I would have written more, but couldn't. My phone was ringing.
It was my mother.

"Hey there," I said, as if nothing significant had happened.

My mother got straight to the point.

"Imogene, what's going on?"

"You've been watching the news?"

"Yes. Talk to Aunt Clara."

My Aunt Clara is a very tiny person with a disproportionately large voice. One has no right to expect the booming sound that comes from her throat.

"Imogene, sweetie, what's going on? On TV, they said you've carrying on with that dead writer in Houston. And you just got there!"

"I've been here about a month now. But that's not the point. Don't believe what you hear on the news."

"You mean it's not true?" She sounded almost disappointed.

"Completely untrue. I've never met the man. Besides, I don't think he's—" but I stopped. The information that George Zimaresh was not really dead (in my opinion) was what you'd call confidential. Telling Aunt Clara would be equivalent to broadcasting it to the state of Alabama (at the very least).

"Don't think he's what, dear?"

"I was saying I don't think he's—he's—"

"Yes, dear, you're not enunciating properly."

"What I meant was that I don't think he's really a Mormon." It sounds silly, I know, but this is the first thing that came into my head.

"Mormon? They never said anything about him being a Mormon."

"Well, at least they got that right."

"But darling, why are you babbling about Mormons? Talk to Aunt Clara…"

"There's nothing to talk about. I wasn't going around with this Zimaresh guy. I'm just the pathologist investigating the case."

But Aunt Clara was more interested in my tragic love affair. "Here, talk to your mother."

"Now, Imogene," said my mother, trying to sound like my best friend, "You know we're here for you. You can tell us anything."

"Mama, there's nothing I'd like to do more. But this is the truth. I've never met this guy. There's nothing to tell."

"But then why does everyone think—"

"They've got it wrong, mother. I don't know why, but Zimaresh has been sending me letters. Maybe that's why they think what they think about me. What exactly are they saying?"

"That you may have been a *friend* of his."

"That bad, huh?"

"You know what I mean, Imogene. A *friend*. *That* kind of friend."

"I'm going to sue them, Mama," I said impulsively. "I'm going to make them pay through the nose for spreading rumors about me. They'll be paying me through the nose for the rest of their lives," I said, the heat getting to my brain. Suing these bastards seemed like a wonderful idea to me. It would solve all my money problems.

"Uncle Jerry knows a lawyer in Houston, Imogene," said my mother.

"Well, get me his name, Mama. I'm going to court over this."

No sense in being a passive recipient. There are those who sit quietly while life washes over them like a tidal wave. Others struggle ineffectively. I was going to struggle for a bit.

But first, I had to know what the enemy was saying.

I buzzed Rebecca.

"Yes, dear?" came her soothing voice over the intercom.

"Can you get me a couple of newspapers?"

23

I need not have asked for the newspapers. It was all over the web.

Bizarre murder of famous mystery writer, was the title of one.

Another one:

Zimaresh dead at fifty-four. An unbelievable murder.

And the one that I found most relevant:

Fact or Fiction? Murdered mystery writer may have been pathologist's lover.

I clicked on the link for this story and found myself reading a fictional account of what really happened.

Famous writer George Zimaresh was found brutally beheaded in his study. Police find themselves at a loss to explain how his murderer could have escaped from the locked room in which Zimaresh was found. Police sources indicate that the murder may have been commissioned by the author himself. Zimaresh is no stranger to the world of murder, being the author of bestselling murder mysteries such as Murder in a Delicatessen *and* Murder Never Takes a Holiday. *Most of his mysteries feature the gourmet detective Maximilian Joyce. His books have sold over twenty million copies.*

Whatever the reason behind this bizarre death, it is known that he left a letter at the crime scene addressed to a forensic pathologist investigating this case, Dr. Imogene Chaplin. Dr. Chaplin came to Houston a month ago. She is a part-time medical examiner. A source in the medical examiner's office has hinted that Dr. Chaplin and Mr. Zimaresh may have been lovers. Dr. Chaplin has not been reached for comment.

I read again:

A source in the medical examiner's office has hinted that Dr. Chaplin and Mr. Zimaresh may have been lovers.

What?

What *source*?

I read on:

Activity on the official Zimaresh website, <u>www.Zimaresh.com</u>, has exploded. Booksellers across the country indicate that sales of Zimaresh books have suddenly escalated. In a strange coincidence, his last completed novel, Murder Me, Murder You, *is expected to hit the stores tomorrow. Ironically,* Murder Me, Murder You *is said to be a classic locked room murder mystery, in which a mystery writer is found killed in a room that no one could have left without leaving the door unlocked. Orders for this book have multiplied several-fold. His daughter, Amelia Zimaresh, has confirmed that she will appear on a TV special tonight, as planned, to promote her own book,* My Good Bad Dad.

I was aware of a strange buzz inside my head. What was it? I guess it was some sort of intuition or sense of why Zimaresh had turned into a murderer.

I had stumbled upon a motive. The oldest motive in the world.

Money.

24

Money.

It drives men and women to extraordinary lengths. *What* won't most people do for money? I mean, of course, the right amount of money. Oh, I admit most people wouldn't kill their only child for money, and I'm sure all of us can think of a few things that we would never do for any price. Apart from these few things, the right price can be guaranteed to make us do practically anything.

So Zimaresh, with twenty million copies in print, was set to sell millions more. His last novel, "Murder Me, Murder You," *about to be released tomorrow,* was about a mystery writer killed in a locked room. Simply a coincidence? Or a method of boosting sales? It's not every day that your favorite mystery writer is killed in a similar manner as described in his novel. He doesn't even have to be your favorite writer—and you'll still go to the bookstore and get a copy—just out of curiosity.

So, Zimaresh stood to gain a lot of money. But he already had a bunch of money, right? He could still want more, however. Can one ever have enough? The world economy would collapse tomorrow if people stopped being nice and greedy.

There was another logical objection to the he-did-it-for-money hypothesis. How would Zimaresh get access to his millions? If he wasn't alive, he couldn't touch it, and if he was alive, his money would pass to his heirs, and he still wouldn't be able to touch it. But he'd already shown himself to be a very clever man. Couldn't he have figured out some sneaky legal loophole to get to his cash?

The more I saw it, the more it seemed like the correct motive.

Zimaresh dies.

His book comes about a day or two later—with the exact same topic.

And, consider the last sentence in the article I've quoted: *His daughter, Amelia Zimaresh, has confirmed that she will appear on a TV special tonight, as planned, to promote her own book,* My Good Bad Dad.

An appearance planned on TV. And carried on as scheduled. How many of us, discovering our father had been beheaded, would show up on a TV show?

I suppose one could, for the right price.

25

Meanwhile, I had a call from the lab.

"You want to come take a look at this?"

This is how lab people sometimes talk. They skip the intro and jump straight to the point. So what if this process is confusing? At least time has been saved.

"Come take a look at *what?*" I barked.

"The blood sample."

See what I mean? The blood sample. Which one? The un-clotted blood found in the *lota* and the study? Or the one scraped from the workroom behind the study, where the victim was killed? I didn't know. I patiently decided not to ask any questions. The truth would emerge from behind this veil of confusion if only I was patient and didn't try too hard to make sense of Marisa's remarks.

"It's very well preserved. I had to call the new Metropolitan Zoo in Houston, though."

"I see, the Metropolitan Zoo." I sighed. "And I'm assuming, Marisa, that you had an excellent reason to call the Metropolitan Zoo."

"Yes," said Marisa, without any emotion. "I'd been at the zoo with Clarissa, my niece, and they now have a camel, which was interesting because they've never had a camel at the Metropolitan Zoo."

"This gets more and more fascinating," I muttered, half to myself, half into the phone. "I see, so now they have a camel at the Metropolitan Zoo. Which kind?"

I asked because I suddenly remembered that there are those with one hump and those with two humps, and one of them comes from India and the other from Africa or Arabia.

"Which kind? I don't remember. Clarissa threw up, and so I didn't have time to read the information on it."

"It doesn't matter," I said, irritated that I had allowed myself to wander off. "Please go on. I remember we said that there was a camel at the zoo—"

"Yes, and what's more interesting, they have another camel, a baby one, who had an accident and lost some blood. So they got some camel blood flown in from, oh, I don't remember where. But the point is, they got in some camel blood a couple of days ago, several bags of it, and many of them went missing."

"Missing?" My ears pricked up at this. Now, I began to see, though very vaguely, where Marisa was drifting with this.

"Yes, missing. That's what I called the Zoo about. I didn't know they were missing, but I had a hunch, so I called the Zoo, and they told me that the blood had definitely gone missing—not all of it, thank God, because the baby camel would've died."

"And now, will you tell me why you had this hunch?" I had to coax the information out of her. What if I died before this conversation ended? I'd never know what the hell she was babbling about.

"Oh! Didn't I say? The blood you collected at the scene, the unclotted sample, it has oval red cells."

Oval red cells.

"It's possible that the deceased individual had anemia—you know, of course, Doctor Chaplin, that some people with certain types of anemias can get oval cells, but I'll bet you a latte that this is camel blood."

"Camel blood," I repeated.

"Camel blood. Camels have oval red cells. It's difficult to tell because the blood is not fresh, and it was at room temperature and exposed and all that, but it was whole blood, and so I can see under the microscope that it has oval red cells, just like a camel's."

Whole blood refers to the kind of blood we were dealing with. When blood is transfused, mostly components of blood are used, like packed red cells, white cells, or platelets; whole blood, that is to say, blood that has not been split into components is very rarely given nowadays—only in certain special situations that I can't remember. Or if you're a camel, I suppose. I confess I don't know much about camel medicine.

26

Camel blood.

I sighed, trying hopelessly to make sense of this case.

Why steal camel blood?

Why?

Because camels have oval red cells, it is possible to tell them apart from human red cells. Clue number five from his first letter to me: *Number five: The blood—quite a bit of it, wouldn't you agree?*

Yes, quite a bit of it, *and not belonging to the dead man*. Rightfully belonging to a poor camel, but stolen and then sprinkled on the scene. Zimaresh had to make sure we figured out that the blood didn't belong to the dead man. What better way than to steal some *camel* blood?

But what a coincidence! A baby camel with an accident needing camel blood; camel blood flown over; camel blood stolen. If Zimaresh had been planning this murder—and it was obvious that he had spent quite a bit of time planning it—then he couldn't have just relied upon a camel having a fortuitous accident to set this chain of events in motion.

In other words, Zimaresh had to make sure that he would be able to help himself to camel blood. He couldn't have just thought of this on the spur of the moment.

It was time to do some sleuthing. I picked up the phone to call Helen Freud.

Rebecca kept pushing little notes to me. Most of these were from some news station or radio station or a paper asking for some kind of comment. I had no comment except to say, Piss Off, but I couldn't just say that. I have a healthy fear of the media, and even though a part of me wished to yell at them, threaten to sue the hell out of them, etc., another, more fearful part advised caution. Only trouble happens to people who mess with the news machinery. The news can make you look like a corrupt or stupid monster. (Which would I pick, stupid or corrupt? People can forgive corruption if you repent, but if you're stupid, you stay stupid. So, it is a tough choice. But that is not the point: Neither is particularly attractive to a single pathologist hoping to succeed in the world.)

The wisest course of action was to say nothing at all. No comment is an acceptable stance—that is to say, acceptable to the media. They understand the game of "no comment." In my opinion, the juiciest bait for the media is the "no comment." It makes them salivate like mad, and they get even more eager to break the story. Also, they are less likely to publish bad stuff about you. They may hope that you'll speak eventually, and if you do, you're more likely to talk to someone who hasn't insulted you. At least that's my naïve view, gathered from years and years of watching TV and reading newspapers.

So I told Rebecca the standard reply to give to these news-hungry savages: No comment.

One of the messages was from Roy Culpepper. You remember Roy Culpepper? He was my boss at the private pathology group where I was working part-time. I felt the familiar sinking feeling in the middle of my abdomen—it's the kind of feeling that is described as a pit in the stomach, a sort of churning, achy feeling like somebody is pouring acid and burning a hole in your stomach. Needless to say, an unpleasant sensation. Why was Roy Culpepper calling me? To congratulate me on my recent notoriety? Hardly likely.

It was as I had suspected.

"Imogene," he said, sounding almost nervous.

"Yes, Roy?"

"This thing in the news—about the dead mystery writer and you…"

"It's not true, not true at all."

"Not true?" Did I detect disappointment in his voice?

"Complete nonsense."

"I don't know—we have to discuss this. Labs are a vicious business—very competitive, as you are aware. We're not like Hollywood—we don't crave bad publicity."

"Look, Roy," I said, trying to erase the fear from my voice. "This thing will blow over in a few days. Right this minute, I'm preparing a statement for the media," I lied.

"A statement?"

"Yes. To the effect that there was nothing, ever, between me and Zimaresh. Ever. I'll threaten to take them to court."

"Court?" Roy sounded uncertain.

"Why not? The supreme court, if need be."

"Hmm," said Roy.

One more thing to worry about. My job. My potentially lucrative job. The way I sensed it, I wasn't going to have any such job. Roy Culpepper sounded like he didn't want his lab to be anywhere near me.

Everything happening at the same time—did it have to be like this? Well, it was. And the only thing I could do was to think.

27

Think.

There were two major problems with this whole business, from my point of view.

Number One: Zimaresh had somehow magically managed to decapitate his victim and then disappeared from the inside of a locked room, taking the head and the weapon with him. Now, of course, that was impossible. So impossible that the murder couldn't have happened the way we thought it had. In other words, Zimaresh had either left through some other way or through the door, somehow locking the door behind him. But what was this other way? As far as I, or anybody, could tell, there was no other way. There were the two trees connected by the underground tunnel, but these were designed in such a way that you could only lock the tree door only from inside the trunk; and the tree outside the room was locked, and the tree inside the room was unlocked—in other words, if Zimaresh had used the trees, *he had come from the outside in*. This was the *opposite* of what he should have done if he really wanted to get out of the room. The conclusion was that he had not left through the trees. He could not have escaped through the passageway behind the bookshelves. That was a blind loop—the passage led only to the workroom inside, where the murder had actually taken place. There was no way out from there.

So, the only way out for him was through the front door of the study. And that was locked from the inside.

Was it some funny business to do with the lock? I mean, was it possible for someone to somehow lock it from the outside even though it seemed that one couldn't lock it from the outside? Maybe a lock with a code or mechanism of some kind that made this kind of action possible. Highly unlikely, I thought. Experts were busy examining the lock, and we'd soon know for sure. But I strongly suspected it could be something as easy as a "funny" lock, with a sneaky way of locking it from the outside. Zimaresh, the mystery writer, had planned the impossible murder. If you could cheat with the lock, it would take the challenge of apparent impossibility away. This is not the kind of murder a famous mystery writer would leave behind as his final, great puzzle.

No, this was the *impossible* murder. The solution had to be a possible one, naturally, but hidden so completely that it seemed impossible.

Somehow, Zimaresh had walked through the front door without anyone noticing. Maybe he was already in the room when we had entered it, but that was impossible. We would've seen him, right?

Impossible! Impossible! Impossible! At the risk of sounding like the proverbial broken record, or CD, or iPod, let me say it again: Impossible!

So that's where we were. The only logical time for Zimaresh and friend with sword and head to have left the room was right when the door was opened—by a bunch of cops!

And by a very large number of cops at that. Another one of his incomprehensible clues. If you want to escape, why make sure that you have so many police officers on the scene?

28

So much for problem number one.

Problem number two was more personal and, therefore, more important to me. It was this: Zimaresh had left letters addressed to me.

Me.

Now, had I been a famous pathologist, this might have been understandable. Criminal masterminds want their work appreciated and probably try to attract the attention of respected individuals in the field of criminology. But I wasn't that person. I was barely out of training, a junior pathologist. Nobody knew me. But Zimaresh had. He had left me letters. This was problem number two, and it was a damn difficult one.

I had been in Houston for hardly a month. Prior to that, I'd been in Potokapaw, a university town in the south of Alabama—had Zimaresh come to know me there? No, that was ridiculous. Even if he'd known about me there, he had no way of knowing I'd ever show up in Houston one day in time for his grand exit. And exactly why would he be interested in me, anyway? Somebody so inexperienced and raw that she could hardly take the right step without someone holding her hand?

Another dead end.

As you can see, this bout of thinking was going nowhere. I was exactly where I had started.

With a sudden inspiration—I think it was an inspiration because this led to a major breakthrough in the case for me (even though I didn't realize it at the time)—I accepted the fact that I couldn't—just couldn't—get inside Zimaresh's head to figure out exactly why he had selected me to be the recipient of his irritating (and frightening) letters. I couldn't understand it. And I suddenly became comfortable with that in a Zen sort of way. You know, there are times when you are just banging your head against a brick wall, and the only thing certain is that you're going to end up with a bad headache or a broken head. The thing to do if you find yourself in that situation is to stop it. That's it. Stop it. And so I did. I stopped it.

When I did, a tiny inspiration broke through. It was nothing major, but then, I'm not Albert Einstein.

I realized that it was more important for me to understand *how* he had stumbled upon me. The *how*, not the why.

Here's my reasoning: Zimaresh was not a gifted psychic, filled with the second (or is it third?) sight. So he had to go about some way, some *physical* way, involving a human being, most likely, who could tell him about me. Someone to tell him, Look, here's this pathologist, her name is Imogene Chaplin. *That* was the only way he'd found me out and then written letters to me.

Someone had told him about me. Perhaps innocently. Or perhaps not so innocently; maybe a spy, someone working for him, or working *with* him. Someone working with him and working with me at the same time, here, at the medical examiner's office.

Could that someone be—and here you will see how paranoid I'd become—could that someone be Felicity Moon? I know, you think I'm being ridiculous, and maybe I was being ridiculous, but it was a logical thought on my part. Felicity Moon may have been working with him. Felicity Moon was now also dead. Why? To silence her, perhaps, so that she wouldn't give him up?

Ridiculous.

Once again, I had that hopeless feeling of getting nowhere, but I kept thinking about the *how*. And I came up with at least one more thing to add to my to-do list.

To check if Felicity Moon was a friend of Zimaresh—the man had several lady friends, so why not Dr. Moon?

Felicity Moon. A friend? Or a lover?

The little green book, I thought.

29

All thoughts and all considerations were put on hold. Amelia Zimaresh, the author of *My Good Bad Dad* and the daughter of her father, George Zimaresh, was at the morgue.

Truth be told, I was curious. People are often curious about the children of famous people. As we see them, we often wonder, what's it like to be the child of someone so famous? As people constantly approach your mum or dad for an autograph, as others fawn over your parents, as your parents appear on TV, and their photos in newspapers or magazines? Does it get very tiresome after a while? Does the child get a complex or anxiety, wondering if she'll ever be that famous?

Amelia Z. turned out to be a stunning woman in her early thirties. I don't know why, but I was surprised. She was curvaceous in the way that I'm not, and she reminded me vaguely of a face I'd seen before. Of course, George Zimaresh himself! I'd seen photos of him on the back of his books. She looked like him a bit. A narrow face, but attractive, eye-catching.

"May I see him?" she asked.

The body was displayed to her.

She shook her head.

"As I suspected! Oh damn, what's Daddy done!"

I raised an eyebrow.

"What exactly do you mean?"

"This man—it's not Daddy. Can we go somewhere else? I don't want to keep staring at this poor man."

"Of course."

I led her out of her room and into Alec Spence's office.

She dabbed her eyes. I didn't know why because her eyes seemed completely dry to me.

"There's something in this room," she said irritably. "It's not agreeing with my contacts."

"I'm sorry. Would you prefer if we moved elsewhere?"

"No, no, let's get done with it."

"I suppose you've got to get ready for the interview tonight."

"Yes, naturally. It's a live TV special devoted to my dad, and I have fifteen minutes on it. And I had to make sure before I said it."

"Said what?"

"What I suspected. I knew Daddy wasn't dead. It didn't make sense to me."

"Why not? But first, how can you be sure it's not your father."

"The mole on his knee. He had a hideous one that he was very proud of. He was like that."

"You're sure he had a mole…which knee?"

"Am I sure? Are you sure of your name? Is the Pope really sure there is a God?" She came dangerously close to snorting. "Naturally, I'm sure! I may not have spent every minute of the day with him, but I know that he had a mole. It was on his left knee."

"He could've had it removed."

"That mole?" She sounded dumbfounded, as if I'd said the most idiotic thing in the world. "He loved that mole. In fact, when I asked him— while working on my biography of him—why he didn't have that ugly thing taken out, he told me—you know what he told me?"

I shook my head.

"He told me, 'I'm going to leave it right where it is, in case you ever have to identify me.'"

"What a strange thing to say…"

"Not if you were Daddy. Daddy said the strangest things, only they sounded totally ordinary when they came out of his mouth."

"When did he say that to you?"

"Let me see…several months ago, maybe three—four—or five, something like that."

Three—four—or five months.

So he'd been planning this for at least that long—it was also that long since he'd been diagnosed with terminal cancer. He'd left the mole so that we'd know *for sure* that the headless corpse wasn't his. Unless Amelia was wrong. She could be lying, couldn't she? If she went on TV and said, "That's not my dad," people would go mad. The publicity blitz would go wild. More and more people, like trained seals, would dive into the bookstores, buying his books—and her book as well.

"Were you at the party yesterday?"

For a moment, she was silent. Then, after a pause, she said, "Yes."

Why the pause?

"Were you expecting something to happen?"

She was silent again. I realized that I didn't like this woman very much, but in these moments of silence, she seemed almost human.

"Yes," she said. "I don't know what to say…"

"Why don't you please say something, something that'll clear this foggy problem for me? He's been leaving me all these letters. Look, it will really help," I said with unusual honesty and a bit of desperation. I don't often unburden my woes to all and sundry, but I wanted to get to the bottom of this—simply for my own peace of mind.

"Yes, I know. I've read the news. I just assumed the two of you were—" she bit her lip.

"No," I said. "We weren't involved. I didn't even know him—I mean, I knew he was a famous author, and I've read some of his novels, but I didn't know him. Imagine my shock that he's been leaving me letters on how to solve the mystery of how he was killed!"

"That's typical," she said. "Him doing things like that. It's a mystery, you see, a real-life mystery. He planned it, I've been sure of it from the very beginning. I'm sorry you got in the middle of this," she sounded nearly sincere. "I think I've got to tell you something."

30

"Daddy was not a nice man."

She shrugged her shoulders.

"Don't get me wrong; I loved him, and he loved me, but for the longest time, he didn't show it. He was nasty to me, but then he was also very sweet to me—at different times, of course. When I say nasty, I mean really nasty. If you're interested, you should check out my book, *My Good Bad Dad*. It hits the stores today."

I could barely believe she was promoting her book at this point. I've often heard that authors, especially ones who are not well known, lose no opportunity to announce their books in the most appealing terms to all who will listen. But I don't believe she needed my support to make her book a bestseller. Her father's actions had made sure that her book would make it rise to the very top of the bestseller list—right behind her father's latest book, *Murder Me, Murder You*.

"We've had a very rocky relationship. I won't bore you with the details of my horrible life. It's not that boring, I hope. I think it's a pretty interesting story. And as I describe in my book, it's a story of redemption. I think, in the end, my father redeemed himself, at least in my eyes. Some months ago, Daddy discovered that he had cancer. It was in his brain, but it was coming from somewhere else—it was a metastasis. The doctors couldn't tell where it was coming from—isn't that strange? What's the point of being a doctor if you can't even tell where the cancer's coming from? But that's beside the point. The prognosis was grave. His doctor couldn't be sure but gave him three to six months. As far as I could see, it didn't affect his thinking, but it's not good to have cancer gallivanting all over your brain coming from who-knows-where."

No, definitely not good.

"The cancer did something to him. I think it gave him an attack of conscience of an odd sort. He called me one day and asked me to see him—immediately. I ignored him. But he kept calling, and so I went to see him. He told me everything, then. He told me he'd lost most of his money—something about his investment advisor being a scum-bag, a real jerk. This advisor lined his own pockets at Daddy's expense and led Daddy down some real losers, risky investments. The net result was that Daddy was not technically poor, but he was very pure compared to what he'd been. I think he lost something in the neighborhood of a hundred million dollars."

A hundred million dollars. My eyes widened.

"I know you're wondering why just a hundred million dollars—maybe you think all famous writers are billionaires," she said with a shrug. Actually, I was not wondering any such thing. From where I stood, a hundred million dollars was a marvelous sum of money. Imagine! A hundred million dollars. Enough to disappear on some island without any worries about crazy authors or pesky reporters or not being able to work and earn as much as pathologists in private practice.

Amelia continued:

"He should've had more. I agree. But Daddy had such a loose hand. He couldn't, just couldn't hold on to money. He had no financial sense. He bought useless things or things that became useless soon after he bought them. He paid a ton to his ex-wives and even paid larger sums of money to his many ex-mistresses! He was a romantic man with savage passions, there's no way to hide this fact—his love affairs alone are covered in two hundred pages in my book! The man was a money-losing machine. If he'd kept his head, he'd be worth half a billion or so, his accountant told him once—and I'm talking liquid cash—not counting property and other assets. His last greatest loss was what he shelled out for the useless investments Mr. Grimald suggested to him. A hundred million dollars. Now, I suppose he probably has a few million in cash. Of course, if you add all his houses and property, you're probably talking some millions more, but that's nothing for a man like him. A man who was worth so much more."

I blinked. "Some millions more" in assets. A few million in cash. Enough to satisfy me, but obviously not enough to satisfy a hungrier appetite like that of Amelia Zimaresh.

There was a look of great sadness in her eyes. A look of regret. A half-a-billion dollar inheritance reduced to a measly few million.

I thought I knew how she felt. I felt something similar after I bought something nice but stupid at the mall. The feeling of I-wish-I-hadn't-wasted-my-money-on-something-so-silly. Except, in her case, somebody else, her father, had squandered her inheritance.

I'm sure *that* felt much worse.

31

"He told me he was going to make amends. He had a new novel coming out. An impossible locked room mystery about a man murdered inside a locked room. He said it was the second-best thing he'd ever written."

My ears pricked up at this. "Second-best?"

"Yes. The best thing, he said, would come afterward. A real-life mystery, one that had himself as a character. I asked him what he meant, but he told me to be patient."

She was silent for a moment.

"I insisted he tell me. After a while, he said that it was his grand design to redeem his fortune. He felt bad that he had made such stupid decisions and that *I* would suffer for his stupidity. He apologized to me. 'But don't worry,' he told me, 'I have a plan.' For starters, there was a made-for-TV movie about his life (for which I served as one of the consultants). It comes out this weekend."

This weekend. Again, how convenient!

People would be glued to their TV sets, eager to find out about this mysterious mad genius who'd designed such a mind-boggling real-life crime. I often think it is we, the consuming public, the citizens of our crazy world, who are the real criminals. We encourage criminals with our attention and our dollars. The world can be yours today if you do something sufficiently nutty or dreadful—something that is considered newsworthy.

"His publicist and agent, Richard Shell, came up with the idea of a TV movie about Daddy. He thought of it after he saw an actor. That's what gave him the idea. He'd seen this actor on stage—he'd performed at a local theater in Houston. He was struck by how much like Daddy this actor looked."

Now, that was something!

An actor who looked like Daddy.

Maybe also an actor who was dead without a head in Daddy's study.

A crazy idea?

Why?

It was logical. Zimaresh needed a corpse that would be similar to him, similar in size and shape, that is. Naturally, Zimaresh couldn't leave the head behind because the actor was the actor, not Zimaresh. This was a plausible reason *why* the head was missing (even if we couldn't figure out *how* it was missing).

She looked me straight in the eyes.

"I hate to have to say it, but I think Daddy planned all this because he wanted his book sales to go through the roof. My book sales, too. As I mentioned, my book comes out. Already, there's a buzz going with people lining up to buy it. My publisher called me this morning telling me that they'll have to print many more copies urgently. Daddy has a publishing house—it publishes his novels, as well as mysteries by other, long-dead authors—only those authors to whom you don't have to pay royalties."

"And I presume that your father published all his own novels on his own."

"Only except for the first ten or so. He made good money on them, but nothing like after he became really famous and got to keep all the rights and the lion's share of the profits. Publishers would've paid him well but nothing like what he could pay himself."

"Why couldn't he have used his publishing company to recover his money?"

She looked at me in amazement, as if shocked that I couldn't figure out the answer to such a simple question.

"Books make the most money when they come out; then, as time goes on, interest dies down, and fewer copies are sold. Daddy's last novel, *Death of a Sex Therapist,* came out two years ago, and there was a small bump in his previous titles. His new one, which comes out soon, is expected to do very well, but nothing like what it will do now. Now that Daddy's done what he's done, all his books, not just his latest one, will start selling like crazy. Not to mention all the movie deals and the TV serials. Did I mention there's talk of the Zimaresh Mystery Hour, which will show some of his most well-known mysteries?"

"As his principal heir," I said cautiously, "I presume you will get to make all the deals and keep most of the profits."

She looked at me, looking not in the least offended. I guess she liked the idea of keeping the profits.

"There are other parties involved," she said, sounding like a lawyer. "Richard Shell, his agent, publicist, and partner for one. He's a lawyer as well. Then there's the stuff he'll leave for my mother and his other ex-wives. I don't think that he'll leave much for my brother because they hate each other. He almost spat on Daddy the last time they met. But maybe he'll leave him something, maybe he'll leave him a *lot*. I really don't give a damn. But aren't you being premature about this? We know he's not dead, right?"

32

I didn't know what to make of Amelia. Did she really not care? The Zimaresh fortune was going to get a sudden boost thanks to Daddy's homicidal efforts. Amelia herself was going to do extremely well with her book about her "good, bad dad."

All this thinking about dads left me wanting to talk to my own, who was sitting in London, studying a rare species of beetle. My parents spend most of the year apart from each other, but they're not really separated. I guess they've reached a level in their relationship where they don't need to talk or spend time together. Anyway, my father, Jonathan Chaplin, who's as English as you can get, suddenly discovered the hidden depths of beetles after retirement and now spends most of his time trying to discover a new, undescribed species of beetle. Will he find one? Who knows? But at least he's having a jolly good time in his quest.

"Hullo, my dear," said my father in his deep but hushed voice. I immediately felt better. There's something comforting about the old chap. A feeling of it-can't-really-be-that-bad comes over me every time I chat with him.

I filled him in quickly. He already had a very good, if biased, idea of what had happened. My mother had already called him and given him a no doubt hysterical account of my misadventures and shameful behavior. Even if I wasn't really sleeping with the dead mystery writer, it was still my fault. I had no business receiving letters from a crazy writer. Some mothers tend to imagine that it's always all your fault (or theirs, for not bringing you up any better).

But I'm straying away from the point.

My father listened to me with an occasional slurp—I imagine he was having a cup of tea. When I'd finished, he gave his verdict:

"Devilish business, what?"

"Yes, papa, very devilish. I feel the devil's biting my ass."

"The arse, as you say, is the devil's favorite spot. He gets you running in ten different directions all at once. But let's leave the devil out of it, shall we? If you forget about all the other peripheral stuff, this is a fascinating affair, isn't it?"

"Fascinating, yes, but I need help," I sighed.

"But naturally, m'dear. The way I see it, you have one major problem here. Your Mr. Zimaresh—I find his books quite vulgar, I have to say—your Mr. Zimaresh has pulled a fast one on you. He vanished from this room with a man's head, a weapon, and one accomplice. Did I hear you correctly that when you opened the room, he wasn't there?"

"Exactly."

"Impossible. It is impossible unless there is a secret hiding place or something that nobody knows about."

"I seriously doubt it. Helen's checking it out, though. If there's anything, she'll find out. She's a real bulldog."

"Your aunt Miriam used to be like that. Unfortunately, she even smelled like a bulldog. How about your friend, this Helen? Pleasant, odorwise?"

"Papa, we're straying off the subject."

"How right you are, m'dear. I shall focus the mighty Chaplin brain on the problem." There was silence. "Sorry, darling, nothing."

I was about to say something when he spoke again suddenly,

"You know, you have to think simply. Put yourself in this man's shoes. He was no Agatha Christie—he was a truly mediocre talent. Imagine him planning a murder. How complicated can he make it? He lacks the brains for anything too complex, if we can use his writings to judge him."

"But that doesn't help me…"

"But of course it does. Think. A locked room with a headless body. No murderers, no weapon, no head. Where are they? They have to be in the room. Maybe they left the room before you broke into it."

"They couldn't have left the room before we got inside. If they did, how did they lock the room behind them? I tell you, the room was empty of all humans except for the dead man."

"Yes, I know you keep telling me, but that is simply impossible. *Therefore, they had to be in the room*. There's no other way possible, you agree?"

"I agree," I said, feeling more hopeless than ever. "But we didn't see nobody."

"Didn't see *anybody*, dear, but that's beside the point. You didn't see them, but they were there, and you simply didn't see them. It's like a magician's trick. It's all there, right in front of you, but you are tricked into not noticing. In my experience with the common London beetle, they can give you the slip faster than you can blink. But no beetle can escape without escaping—there are no magical beetles—and the same applies to your Mr. Zimaresh. He was there, and he escaped right in front of you, only you weren't looking."

I shook my head. It was wasted on him, naturally, since he was thousands of miles away in an English garden, enjoying a cup of tea and likely gazing adoringly at a common London beetle.

But Zimaresh and his big-footed accomplice were not common London beetles. They were flesh and blood people, many hundreds of times larger than the average beetle. A beetle may whiz past unnoticed. But a man? Or two men? Or one man and one woman? Carrying a bloody weapon and a human head?

No.

Impossible. (There I go again with my constant refrain.)

But it was possible because it had happened. And so, it had to be possible.

So how?

"Nevertheless, my dear, it's just the same as it is with the beetles."

"What is?"

"A murder is."

"How is a murder in any way similar to observing beetles?" I sighed.

"You said it yourself. Observation. Data collection. The murder happened at the party. Well, you must learn everything you can about the party, who was there, and so on. Also, what happened before the party? Maybe Mr. Zimaresh's friend, the one who helped him kill, came before the party? Perhaps your Zimaresh's valet, Perkins, let the accomplice in? Maybe the accomplice was a guest at the party. These are questions that must be answered. Perhaps then you'll see your way through to an idea of some kind."

I thanked him for his advice. But I had little hope I'd find anything at all.

I was wrong.

33

I didn't know Dr. Gopal. After talking to him, I felt like I didn't ever want to talk to him or to anyone again. What was the point of it all? Life was so meaningless, wasn't it? At least, that's the feeling I got after talking to him.

It's not that Dr. Gopal was a bad fellow or anything like that. Not at all. It was just that he was so depressing to listen to. It was his voice, a sad voice, more than the subject matter (which in itself was pretty bad, given that he was a cancer specialist, and with your patients dying right, left, and center, you can't be too cheerful).

"Yes, Mr. Zimaresh," he said. "He went dramatically. Most of my patients die horrible deaths."

"Well…being decapitated is pretty horrible."

"Yes, but quick. Don't think I'm advocating it. But I have to say that the majority of my patients have to be drugged and sedated so heavily that sometimes you don't even notice that they've died. It stops the pain, but sometimes it seems much more horrible to me. It can be drawn out over such a long time. Now, Mr. Zimaresh, he went out, pouf! in an instant." He paused. "I'm assuming from what I've read in the paper that he commissioned his own death."

"Well…"

"I know, you probably can't say right now, but I understand why a man would want to go quickly—rather than slowly, painfully, terribly. Don't think of him as a criminal for wanting to take his own life. He didn't have much left."

"Oh, how much then?"

"He had advanced cancer."

"That was when?"

"When—oh, about four, no three, months ago. That's when we found out about it—he's probably had it lurking inside of him."

"How'd he take it?"

"Well. Fairly well. When you gotta go, you gotta go, he told me. Everybody's gotta go one day, and so today is as good as any other day. His words. He sounded stoic or like a Buddhist to me."

A Buddhist? Highly unlikely. What kind of Buddhist goes around decapitating people?

"What kind of cancer was it?"

"I don't know. Multiple small tumors in the brain—adenocarcinoma," he said. Adenocarcinoma is a cancer that forms glands. It was obviously coming to the brain from somewhere else, the primary site.

Dr. Gopal continued: "The trouble was, we couldn't find the primary."

"Oh," I said.

Oh, indeed. Sometimes tumors suddenly pop up in a place, clearly coming from somewhere else, without the primary site ever being found. Perhaps the tumor started in one organ, which is called the primary, for example, the lung, then disappeared or regressed from the primary site, and then showed up, sometime later, in the secondary organ as metastases. It can sometimes be very hard, if not impossible, to figure out where the tumor originated.

Regardless, with multiple tumors in the brain and multiple metastases, the situation for Zimaresh was bad.

"I am assuming you searched everywhere for the tumor."

"Scanned him from head to toe, so to speak," said Dr. Gopal. "But we couldn't find it."

"And the pathologist?"

"The pathologist…" he sighed. "He tried hard, gave his best guess, and said it was probably coming from the colon. Only problem was that

Mr. Zimaresh's colon was clean as a whistle. No sign of a tumor there or in the lungs. Or anywhere else that we could find."

"So what's the prognosis in these kinds of cases, you know, unknown primary, with brain metastases?"

"Well, it would depend on the original tumor, of course, and it is never possible to be completely specific about these things—in my opinion, at least. But it wasn't very long, probably less than a year. Or, it could be three or six months. Not long. That's what I told him. I put it plainly to him. I said he had some time, but not a whole lot, and that he better put his affairs in order."

"And you say he took this news well?"

"Well, obviously, he wasn't jumping with joy. But he took it well, better than I would have. He was a bit gloomy at first. He told me he had a lot of things to take care of. I couldn't tell him to look on the bright side, naturally, because there was no bright side. You get cancer, and it sucks. There's no way to make it any less bad."

A thought went through my mind. I had just figured out a perfect way of proving that the headless body we were dealing with did not belong to Zimaresh.

"Listen, Dr. Gopal—"

"Please call me Gopi."

"Of course, Gopi...the tissue that was used to make the diagnosis. Can we have it?"

"You mean the pathology blocks?"

He was referring to the process whereby tissue removed by the surgeon—in this case, Zimaresh's brain biopsy—is processed by the lab, by the pathologist, and put through a slew of chemicals, including formalin, and turned into a paraffin block that has the tissue in it. Paraffin is a wax. This way, it is easy to cut slices or sections of the tissue, thin four- or five-micron slices that are then stained with certain dyes to give them color. This is what the pathologist sees through the microscope to make his diagnosis. In many cases, the pathologist may have to use other dyes or various antibodies to help her diagnose the case.

In my mind, the beauty of the block was the fact that it contained, without a shadow of a doubt, tissue from George Zimaresh's body. Here we had, no matter how small it was, something that had undoubtedly come from his body. This tissue had something that was invaluable for me—at this point in time.

I mean DNA.

DNA. Deoxyribonucleic acid is the code that tells our body to become what it becomes. If not for the human DNA inside us, you or I could be aardvarks or gibbons.

So, DNA.

George Zimaresh's DNA.

I had a whole body, minus the head, that was full of DNA. It was the easiest thing in the world to take some tissue off the body, grind it up, and process it to yield its DNA. The only problem with the DNA we got was that it was practically useless. Why? Because we had nothing to compare it with. How could we know that it belonged to a specific person, in this case, George Zimaresh? The only way was to *get some tissue that we were certain belonged to Zimaresh, get the DNA out of it, and then compare it to the DNA we got from the body*. If the DNA was the same, we would have a match, and we'd know whose body we had. If I wanted to prove that the body in the study didn't belong to Zimaresh, I needed the tissue block of Zimaresh's brain biopsy to prove it.

"You know, it's odd you should mention it," said Dr. Gopal. Uh-oh. That didn't sound good. Whenever somebody says something like, "It's odd you mention it," chances are that you're going to hate whatever you hear after that.

Dr. Gopal continued, "The funny thing is that a month ago, Mr. Zimaresh called and asked the Pathology department to release all his tissue to him."

"And—"

"Well, pathology had to do it naturally. His tissue belongs to him."

"Yes, of course." Much as pathologists hate parting with it, tissue is the property of the patient. We have no right to keep as much as a speck of any patient's tissue against the patient's wishes.

"Am I to infer from your remark that you don't have his tissue?"

"That about sums it up."

34

Up against a dead-end again.

But it was very interesting, nevertheless. It was obvious that Zimaresh had anticipated this step. It all made sense from the following point of view: *Zimaresh was hell-bent on removing any way of confirming that the body we had found in his room was not actually his.* We could speculate all we wanted. But we wouldn't know for certain.

Anyway, this was hardly the only problem in my life. There was Roy Culpepper, the senior partner in the pathology group I was hoping to join. Roy Culpepper, the lip-licker, was, as I finished my conversation with Dr. Gopal, waiting outside my office.

I took a deep breath. This was serious. He wouldn't have trekked in the treacherous Houston heat through the kind of traffic that makes even pacifists take to violence unless he had a damn good reason to do so. Perhaps he was here to tell me, as kindly as he could, that I was fired.

All in all, the situation demanded several deep breaths. Consequently, I inhaled, patted my hair, and opened the door.

I caught him, his tongue flicking over his lower lip, looking giddy and nervous. A strange look, I have to note. A look I couldn't read very well.

It took him a few moments of staring at me before any sounds emerged from his throat. It was an odd sound, like a frog with a fly stuck in its throat. Mercifully, he followed this emission with recognizable human speech.

"Imogene!" he burst out and slapped his palms on my table. (Actually, my boss, Dr. Spence's table.) He rapped it with such force that he toppled a small figurine of a complacent Buddha. He followed this with many apologies and remarks of an incomprehensible nature. Finally, he ran a hand over his hair, forced his face into a smile, and said, "I don't want to be personal or anything, but do you like older men?"

I was too stunned to reply. He took advantage of my silence to continue as follows:

"I ask, I mean, I am bold enough to ask, because you liked Zimaresh, and he and I, well, we're practically the same age. And I'm not that bad-looking. In fact, most people are always telling me how good I look for, for a man my age, I mean, which is not that old."

He breathed heavily and looked straight into my eyes, with a pained expression on his face, as if he were severely constipated. I must confess I didn't say anything. I merely gaped at him, taken aback by his remarks.

"Things are not good between Mary and me. You know, you have so many dreams in life, you get married, you settle down. But then you get older, and the magic's not there anymore."

I finally found my voice.

"Are you proposing to me?"

"Only something for your consideration. I don't want to put you under any pressure or anything. Just think about it. It has nothing to do with your job with our group. You can slap me on my face and tell me to get the hell out of here if you like. It will have no impact on the group's decision to keep you. I don't want you to think this is sexual harassment or anything like that."

Yeah, right.

"We could grow to like each other. I already like you, Imogene—a lot. You're quite something. I've always seen you as something special. I knew George Zimaresh, you know. I mean, I didn't know him, but I've read a couple of his books. Great writer. He could've written to any woman he liked, and he chose you. Shows you've got it."

"It?"

"A quality. A special something. In someone special." He dropped a meaningful pause, meeting my gaze, while I tried my best to dodge it.

"Listen, you probably think I'm old enough to be your father. Well, I'm not. I'm only fifty-two. I am healthy. I'll probably live till I'm ninety. My grandfather nearly lived to a hundred, and so did my dad. Health is in my genes. I'm still a young man at heart. Even if you did something with Zimaresh, well, it's okay. I don't condemn you. The heart has its own language, right? You got to do what your heart tells you to do."

As you may imagine, this was unexpected. I was appropriately stunned. After several uncomfortable minutes of silence, Culpepper got up suddenly.

"Anyway, that's how I feel. I'll leave you now. You've got your hands full with this case. Just think about what I've said, will you?"

35

But I didn't have any time to think. There was a lot going on. So much so that the occasional inappropriate sexual advance hardly registered inside my head. It would register later on. But I will get to that when the time comes.

Helen was on the phone.

"He was on the board of the Metropolitan Zoo."

As I had suspected.

"He practically forced himself on the board. He gave a fifty thousand dollar donation. Said he was passionate about zoos, nature, animals, etc. Bottom line: he ended up on the board. He was keen that they get the camel, and once they got the camel, he insisted on camel blood."

"Insisted on camel blood?"

"Exactly. Good to have a blood supply handy, he said, in case you had an emergency."

"I see."

"But the board dragged their feet. They said they could get the blood as needed. And they needed it all right because the baby camel had an accident."

"What kind of accident?"

"A puzzling one. Somehow, this kid camel got this bad gash on the side. Nobody knew how. They heard the poor thing bleating like crazy. Then they needed blood in a hurry and got it from somewhere. I've got it right here. Oh hell, my papers are in a mess here, but the point is, they go it, ten bags of it. The baby camel's okay, by the way."

"You're going to tell me about the missing bags, aren't you?" I was impatient.

"I was coming to that. Five bags missing; about two liters or so."

So that was that. The blood mystery was solved. Zimaresh had arranged the whole affair. The wounded camel, the blood. Enough blood for the camel and enough for Zimaresh to spill all over his study.

The message from Zimaresh couldn't have been any clearer: *look, this is not really the victim's blood…this is camel's blood…I engineered the whole thing…I'm your murderer…catch me if you can…*

Helen was onto another topic:

"Oh, by the way, the police business, you remember the clue about the number of police officers?"

"How can I forget? Clue number one: the incredible number of police officers. What about it?"

"Well, Perkins admits to making one 911 call. But then, some of the guests used their cell phones to make more 911 calls. But, it appears that in addition to these, *somebody using Zimaresh's phone* made close to twenty phone calls to individual police officers, begging them to come here."

"And the person who made these phone calls?"

"I'm assuming it was Zimaresh. Calling attention to the crime. First, he commits the impossible crime, then he and his partner escape while there are nearly thirty police officers in his house. It doesn't get any more impressive than that for someone like our psychopathic Mr. Zimaresh."

"Yes. And then his accomplice—the large woman, kills one of our medical examiners, possibly to avoid recognition."

"It seems like that. So we have two killers out loose. And one victim we can't identify."

And that was that.

36

The next item on my agenda was to call Perkins. I wanted to do a bit of sleuthing. But something else happened.

Alex, one of the narcotics lab people, went to the men's room. This could have been a totally dull affair, but it wasn't. Nothing was dull that day. The kind of day when things kept happening. And what happened to Alex was one of those things.

Briefly, then, Alex was complacently doing his business when he caught sight of an unusual object. It was a heavy bust of a Chinese philosopher—in fact, identical to the one he had seen many times in Spence's office. It used to sit on top of a low bookshelf next to the window in his office. Spence is heavily into Buddhist philosophy. Alex also noticed something else. The bust was partly red on the side. Dark red. He went closer to it.

He saw blood. Streaks of dark, red, congealed blood—on the backside of the bust, as if someone had hit somebody else hard with it. And then he saw something else. A bloodstained knife, the kind used in the morgue—in fact, *from* the morgue—*our* morgue.

37

"So the men's room is here, between the front door, where Mr. Spriggs was attacked, and the doctor's offices—where Dr. Moon was killed. Our murderer is a big woman who knocked Spriggs out, then went to your office, Imogene, to leave the letter. She—the killer—was surprised by Dr. Moon and hit her on the head with this heavy statue or bust or what-cha-may-call-it. Then, she went to the morgue, got one of the knives, came back to the office, and stabbed her to death. Then she hid the body under your desk, Imogene. Then she left, presumably by the front door again, where Spriggs was out unconscious."

Helen paused for breath.

"But before she left the morgue, she decided to put the murder weapons, the bust, and the knife in a corner in the toilets, in the men's room where they were found by you." She pointed to Alex, who was clearly enjoying himself. Oh, he had a serious enough expression on his face, but I could sense his palpable excitement. He was obviously one of those who loved being the center of attention—and this stuff with the murder weapons had him as the man of the hour.

He nodded in agreement with Helen's summation.

Simon was already doing his work. The work of gathering the evidence would include analyzing the blood on the knife and the bust. But we didn't need analysis to tell us where the blood had come from—from Felicity Moon.

38

So, Spence was in Denmark. That's a hell of a long way to be away from home, and horrible weather had removed any chance of him being back in time. The earliest he could get out would be the day after tomorrow. Unbelievable as it may seem, this meant that with him in Denmark and Felicity Moon dead, I was the person in charge.

Me!

Ordinarily, there should've been more pathologists working at the medical examiner's office—but there'd been a few problems—budget cuts, people wanting to move, and so on, and the end result was that Spence and Moon were the only two left holding the fort. That's why Spence was forced to get me to help them out. I, or, I should say, someone like me who had minimal experience as a medical examiner.

It was all supposed to be so routine. I would do mostly easy stuff, accidental deaths, falls, etc., and either Spence or Moon was always there for backup when needed. Except now, when Spence was off at a forensic pathology conference in Denmark, and Felicity Moon was no more. Through a peculiar combination of events, "the most incapable person" was "in charge." In case you're wondering why I've used quotation marks, here is the answer:

A letter from that still very much alive George Zimaresh. The only difference from previous letters was that this new letter was not addressed to me. It was one mailed to the Houston Daily News. The editor of one of Houston's most widely circulated newspapers had kindly sent it to me as a courtesy and to get what media people refer to as my "reaction."

Here is the letter:

"Dear Friends,

*How does one go about putting the most incapable person in charge of a difficult case? I found out when I **was told** that a new, very inexperienced pathologist (who is incidentally not even a trained forensic pathologist) was being hired by the Houston Medical Examiner's Office. Here was my chance to test the system. I thought it would be amusing to place before this poor simpleton (note her name: Dr. Imogene Chaplin) a case that even the most experienced investigators would find difficult to solve. Call this my final joke. I put my own death in the bargain. I assure you, it is no easy task to allow yourself to be decapitated. But I did it because life, for me, is now quite meaning-less as I watch the approach of my own impending death. What is better? To die a horrible, drawn-out death in some hospice, all drugged up? Or to go fast, like lightning, under a swift stroke of the executioner's axe?*

*So when I **was told** that this ignoramus (from the forensic point of view) was going to be around, I simply inquired when she would be in town, all by herself, and planned my execution for that time.*

As a mystery writer, I have found that the greater the mystery, the greater the enjoyment for the reading public. Here is my final entertainment. I present my headless body in a locked room from where no one (unless a tiny insect) could escape unnoticed. It is a sufficiently great mystery for those who will rack their brains to find a solution for it. I hope my little offering is appreciated. After all, I've paid for this mystery with my own life.

*But fear not, dear public. The solution will come to you very shortly. I shall provide it myself—I hope you will have the patience to wait. By the way, don't wait for Dr. Chaplin or Detective Freud (another fairly unintelligent human being, from what **I've been told**) to solve this mystery. I've left them a number of clues, including a pretty easy one in this letter, but I won't be surprised if they miss it.*

Until we talk again,

George Zimaresh

A clue. A clue he was sure we would miss. But I didn't, of course, since he had taken the trouble to highlight it several times in the letter.

39

For the time being, I felt it was best not to have a reaction to the media. Or maybe, I wondered, I ought to have some kind of reaction. I reached out to Spence. I was quite controlled, not at all hysterical, which I felt was more than appropriate under the circumstances. Thanks to Zimaresh's newest letter (which would be published in the Houston Daily News), Houstonians would be able to think of me not as Zimaresh's lover but simply as an incompetent, stupid human being. (I didn't know it at the time, but the same letter had been sent to most high-circulation newspapers and to nearly all the big media outfits across the country. Zimaresh's story was big—very big—and it was big because he kept making it bigger. Which was fantastic for his heirs since it meant more and more book sales.)

Spence assured me he was taking the earliest flight imaginable. But it wasn't soon enough. A lot would happen before he arrived. I would come quite close to being dead myself. But I am getting ahead of myself.

"You should say something like, 'we're doing the best we can.'"

"That sounds wimpy," I objected.

"Wimpy is better than saying nothing. If you say nothing, it's admitting you're—er—"

"Incompetent. An idiot," I helped him.

"Something along those lines. You know the media."

(I knew only too well. I've had an unhappy history with the media. Remind me to tell you the story of the naked medical student and the dead homeless people in Potokopaw, Alabama, and how the press somehow turned me into this horrendous, insensitive person. It's a long story, not for now but for another time.)

40

To return to the clue. I want you to take another look at the letter. Here are some parts from it, again:

*How does one go about putting the most incapable person in charge of a difficult case? I found out when I **was told** that a new, very inexperienced pathologist (who is incidentally not even a trained forensic pathologist) was being hired by the Houston Medical Examiner's Office. Here was my chance to test the system.*

And:

*So when I **was told** that this ignoramus (from the forensic point of view) was going to be around, I simply inquired when she would be in town, all by herself, and planned my execution for that time.*

And also:

*By the way, don't wait for Dr. Chaplin or Detective Freud (another fairly unintelligent human being, from what **I've been told**) to solve this mystery.*

As I'm sure you've spotted, he keeps bolding the fragments, "was told" and "I've been told." This was the clue. (Incidentally, here in this letter was an answer to why Mr. Zimaresh had such a great interest in me, why he had singled me out, and why he was leaving me letters all over the place. Clue number seven from his first letter to me was, therefore, clear. Do you remember it? Let me quote you from his letter at the crime scene: *Now you are wondering why I write this to you, isn't that so? You are asking yourself, "I am Imogene Chaplin, a simple pathologist from Potokapaw, and I've never met the* *great George Zimaresh. Why, then, is he writing this letter to me?" Well, this is what we call a <u>clue</u> in the mystery world. Figure out the answer to this one, and you will have figured out the seventh clue I have left for you.)*

The present clue was a simple one. It didn't require a Sherlock Holmes to keep being drawn to the fragments, all of which said the same thing—and which he had bolded so that we wouldn't miss it. **Someone told him** that I was coming to Houston, that I was not really truly a forensic pathologist, and that same someone told him that Detective Freud was incompetent and so on. Who could that someone be?

Well, the list was quite long. Almost anyone at the Houston Medical Examiner's office could have told him. A person working here could have heard all the gossip: who's coming, who's good, who's not, and so on. My paperwork, including the lengthy process of getting a Texas medical license, had been going on for the last five or six months, and I'd been speaking with Spence and various office personnel for at least that long.

So anybody in this office, my office, could have been Zimaresh's liaison, his source, his spy.

I had a flash of intuition, inspiration, or whatever name you want to give it. Because, in an instant, I knew who this someone was. The someone who was not only Zimaresh's spy but the murderer of Dr. Felicity Moon as well.

41

It was around this time, actually shortly thereafter, about an hour or so thereafter, that Lucius Spriggs was found dead, strangled. Another name added to the growing list of victims.

Briefly, Spriggs had checked out of the hospital, against medical advice, I might add. While waiting to get a CT scan on his head, he went to the restroom, but in actuality, he walked out of the hospital in his hospital gown. It was in his hospital gown that he boarded the metro, where he was seen by several concerned passengers, who lost no time in telling the police later on. He was in his hospital gown when he arrived at his midtown apartment. And it was in his hospital gown that he was found strangled inside his apartment. There was no sign of a forced entry. And so, he must have known whoever killed him, someone he had no reason to fear.

Very soon, since I was the only forensic pathologist for miles, I found myself once again at a crime scene. The murders were coming so fast that it was beginning to feel like old hat. Every time I blinked my eyes, it seemed there was yet another murder, yet another crime scene to visit. Very tiresome—and tiring. I was tired, so very tired. But I had to go through the motions.

As you can imagine, the media were drooling with ecstasy. The story got more and more interesting with each passing moment from their point of view. The questions hovering on the minds of the reporters, and which they reported and talked about *ad infinitum, ad nauseam*, were: How would it end? Where was it headed? Who was the homicidal loon or loons behind all this? I can't blame them—can you? This is how those in the media make their living—by telling what happened, where, and when. If nothing happens anywhere, it means no business for them. If the world were one big happy place, with no disease, death, or destruction, very few of us would have anything to do, especially news people. We'd die of boredom, at the very least. In my own profession, the profession of pathology, we get very turned on when we have exciting cases. An exciting case means something unusual, often terrible for the patient, but unusual enough to grab our attention. We often say: "Great case!" in such instances, but it is not a great case for the poor patient, who might conceivably be dead very soon. But we view the world through the peephole of our own perspective, however dreadful it seems to those who don't share our viewpoint.

The same goes for the press. I could blame them for making my job difficult, but I couldn't blame them for doing what they did. They were just humans, like me, and had the same kind of flaws that I had.

Enough philosophizing, though. There was a dead person with a story, a past, that had brought him to this point.

Unlike the other homicides in this case, I knew *exactly* the reason for Spriggs's death.

42

Like most dead bodies I've had the displeasure of seeing, this one was sad and pitiful. Lucius Spriggs, in life, had been a small shrimp of a man and not what you'd call good-looking. Thick, pink, bulbous lips on a small face and a small frame with a tendency to slouch while standing made him a fairly unappealing human being. But at least he was alive when he was alive. Unlike now, dead and helpless, so that anyone could come and do to him what he or she liked.

There were thick red streaks around his neck. I will spare you the details of his face, which resembled the face of any person who has been strangled. From the prettiest movie star to the ugliest human being, they all look the same when strangled. Strangulation is a great leveler.

All forms of murder are terrible, but I find strangulation one of the most disturbing ones of all. Here, the killer has to come close to his victim, so close that he can feel the gasping for air, the pointless clutching, the flailing of the arms and the body, as breath is permanently squeezed out. Hopefully, at some point, the lack of oxygen gets so severe that the victim zones out, perhaps in a pleasant, dreamy state—before being extinguished forever.

Simon, my expert companion and forensic investigator par excellence, pointed to the nails of the victim. They were crusted with reddish-brown dried blood.

"He scratched his killer," I said without much emotion. I was drained, so drained of everything. This was really a lousy job. Being a forensic pathologist is probably okay so long as you don't keep seeing dead people—at least not at the rate I was getting to see them. (Some will disagree with me. Gung-ho forensic people would lose all interest in life if people stopped dying horribly. But the way humans operate, there is little likelihood of that happening.)

My fellow nearly exploded with joy at this point. Did I mention that I had been joined by a trainee forensic pathologist, a sub-optimally perfumed tiny man with disproportionately large hands and thick glasses perched precariously on a bony face? I see that I have forgotten, but I hope you will forgive me since there is so much to mention and record that I can hardly keep track of it all. He was—is—hardly the kind of person you're likely to forget. He looks weird and bright, like a mad scientist, and is unacquainted with deodorants or colognes. But he was and remains a brilliant forensic pathologist (much more brilliant at it than I was—and I was supposed to be one of his instructors in his forensic fellowship!). He was also rather nice and friendly and helpful—in a very intense way. He was one of two fellows that year, doing his forensic pathology fellowship at the Houston Medical Examiners Office. He was returning from his vacation. The other fellow was away interviewing for a job.

His name was Hector. Dr. Hector Malone.

"This will be perfect for collecting DNA samples," he said, appreciatively pointing at the nails with the crusted blood. Blood with DNA—but what would we compare that DNA to? Our chief suspect, the killer Zimaresh, had disappeared without leaving us any samples of his tissue.

"Perfect," I echoed gloomily.

He buzzed about the room like a bee on epinephrine. No detail was too dull for him. He was the prototypical forensic pathologist, the kind you find most often in TV shows and novels. You also find such people in real life; in fact, most members of this profession love their job and are very enthusiastic about it, which is excellent. Can you imagine doing this kind of work any other way, day after day, night after night after day after night, without relishing it in some way?

He took in gusty breaths as if he couldn't get enough of this scene. Personally, I found the aroma in the room less than pleasant. The room was badly ventilated, cheap, and badly needed a few puffs of an air freshener.

"So, what was he strangled with?" he asked, and immediately, like a bloodhound, darted around the room, colliding into Helen Freud in the process.

A quick survey revealed nothing that may have been used to strangle poor Spriggs. That meant nothing, of course. The killer might still have the rope, cloth, and belt used for this purpose. Or he—or she—may have used his own hands. Perhaps this was the same big-footed individual whose footprints we'd found in Zimaresh's study—presumably, this person had big hands as well.

It was about this time that one of Helen's officers handed her an envelope.

"Taped to the backside of a kitchen drawer," he said.

"Hidden there," she editorialized. "But of no future use to him."

She opened it silently. There was a bundle of hundred dollar notes. A pretty fat bundle.

So that was it. Every man, like I've said a thousand times, has his price. And here, in this room, was Spriggs's price: several thousands of dollars—and his life as well.

43

Let me backtrack a bit.

Sitting with a copy of Zimaresh's latest letter, I solved the mystery of Zimaresh's informant in our office and the killer of Dr. Moon.

In his letter, Zimaresh had explained why he had chosen me, someone he didn't know, to communicate with and why he had planned his decapitation to coincide with the time I was on call—and when no one else was around.

He had done so to amuse himself with someone's incompetence (mine, to be precise), to play a ghastly prank, and to earn his heirs a fortune in the process.

He had done so with the help of an accomplice.

An accomplice who worked at the Houston Medical Examiners office.

An accomplice who told him who was who and what was what.

An accomplice who kept him in the loop.

An accomplice who had put a letter from him on my desk.

An accomplice who'd been surprised by Felicity Moon, perhaps in the act of placing Zimaresh's letter.

An accomplice who'd later used a heavy bust of a Chinese philosopher to smash Felicity on the head and had subsequently used a knife from the morgue to kill her.

And an accomplice who'd hidden the bloodied bust and the knife in the *men's* room. *Not* the *ladies* room.

Now recall that Spriggs had told us about a large *woman* who'd hit him, and you'll wonder why this woman had chosen to go inside the men's room. The ladies room was right next to it.

The reason was simple. There was no large woman. The "large woman" was, in fact, a creation of Lucius Spriggs's mind.

I think it was the murder weapons in the men's room that had subconsciously alerted me that Spriggs was lying when he'd concocted the story about the giant female. It made no sense why a woman, who could have easily entered a ladies room, had chosen not to.

Also, Lucius Spriggs had a perfect opportunity to know all the gossip, all the information circulating at the Houston M.E.'s office.

And now, we had discovered several thousand dollars tucked behind a kitchen drawer. This was a very unusual sum of money for a salaried employee, earning next to nothing.

Once I hit upon this thought, my mind analyzed it. It all made sense. Spriggs was Zimaresh's go-between. Zimaresh must have passed him the letter for me, maybe before all this happened or after—it was hard to say. It would have been a simple matter for Spriggs to deliver the letter for me, but it turned out catastrophically. Felicity Moon spotted him, and so Spriggs had to kill her. An unscheduled, unplanned killing. Zimaresh decided to take care of Spriggs in case Spriggs had a sudden attack of conscience and told everything.

I told Freud about my hypothesis—this was before Spriggs made his final exit. She immediately set about to question him, and that was when we found that Spriggs had made his fateful decision to skip the hospital. Maybe he was trying to get the hell out of town. Maybe he was afraid that we'd stumble onto him or, worse, that his master would try to kill him.

Anyway, not finding Spriggs at the hospital, she'd headed to his apartment.

Where he was found. Silenced forever.

44

There were probably ten media vans and about fifty reporters and photographers when I returned to the office. I dodged them with the promise of a press conference, a promise I had no intention of keeping.

In my office, I found that someone had delivered a letter to me. Who had delivered it?

"It was a man," my secretary informed me.

"What kind of man?"

"I don't know. It was very strange. He ran up to the reception but kept looking back, so Milly didn't get a look at his face. He threw the letter in the receptionist's window and then ran away."

Milly was a large, square, silent woman whom I'd seen in one of the offices. She was a temporary replacement for Spriggs at the reception.

But I very much doubted that Milly had any interest in the bizarre behavior of a man who didn't wish to be seen. Milly, from what I could tell of her, seemed an aloof person, detached from the happenings in her surroundings. My guess is that she had probably looked away when she saw this mystery man approach the window, shielding his face from her.

"What was he wearing?" I asked

"A shirt, blue, and pants, black."

"Have you told the police?"

"I told Mr. Simmons."

Mr. Simmons was a general-purpose employee. What I mean is that I don't know what he really did, but whenever someone needed this or that, some kind of job around the office, we sent for Mr. Simmons. It was little surprise to me that he had been elected to communicate information about this suspicious individual to the police. It fit his general job description of an odd-job man.

"Did nobody try to catch him?"

"Mr. Simmons went after him but didn't see him."

This was also hardly surprising since Simmons, a chain smoker, was always wheezing and was not in what could be described as the pink of health. Sending him to chase after someone keen on making a getaway was like getting intoxicated gnats to sing the national anthem, that is to say, a project unlikely to succeed.

But anyway, the point of all this was that I was left with another mysterious letter.

But different from the others.

45

This one was short, to the point, and unlike all the others, handwritten, in a bad scrawl.

If you value your life, get out of here. Don't say in Houston. Get the hell out of Texas. I mean it.

A friend.

Like I said, short and to the point.

I don't know what you make of it, but I made a lot of it. The letter frightened the crap out of me. (It's hardly the time to elaborate on this subject, but I must, in the interest of maintaining physiological accuracy. In actual fact, it is very difficult to frighten the crap out of anyone because in order to get crap out, one has to activate the part of the nervous system that operates when one is *relaxed.* You can *relax* the crap out of someone. When you're frightened, you are naturally not relaxed and so very unlikely to lose control of your sphincter.)

But to return to what I was saying.

I'll tell you what I did. I did something very simple. I picked up the phone to call my secretary.

"Rebecca," I announced in a voice that was shaking, "I'm leaving."

"Okay. Shall I tell them where to get in touch with you?"

I don't know who was the "them" she was referring to. I think she meant just about anyone who wanted to get a hold of me.

"I'm leaving Texas," I said.

Her response was longer in coming this time.

"Oh," she said. "Leaving Texas?"

"Yes," I said.

"When will you be coming back?"

"Never, if I can help it."

I meant it. This job had just crossed from being barely bearable to totally unbearable.

I grabbed hold of a knife from the morgue as I left. A large organ-cutting knife. Do you know what I'm talking about? I mean a very long, 12-inch knife that you use to slice through a dead human's lung, liver, kidney, and so on during an autopsy. Very sharp. I have had occasion to use such a knife in the past—I'll tell you about it someday. It's not a long-range weapon, obviously, but it is excellent for skirmishes at close range (like when someone leaps at you and tries to smother you, as was about to happen to me).

46

I felt a twinge of pain every time I saw my apartment complex. Through some crazy bureaucratic mishap (which means that somebody somewhere screwed up), I was unable to get into the apartment complex I wanted to get into. Houston is a town with a constant turnover of apartments, with new medical residents coming in each July to replace the ones leaving each June. Getting your foot in the door means you've got to be quick. You can't sit on paperwork and hope to get the apartment you want. Somebody screwed up, my application to the apartment was never processed, and so I was on the waiting list to get the first room that became empty.

The complex of my dreams was about a mile away from the M.E.'s office, a gated community with a pool—actually two pools—two gyms, a lavish conference center, covered parking, and complimentary cable. I actually passed this paradise on earth every time I drove to the apartment complex I was living in—a seedy, unkempt horror of a place that faced the road without so much as a shrub to keep unwanted people out. The only advantage to living in these ratty apartments was that they looked cheap and that potential robbers viewed us as totally unsatisfactory as potential victims. I saw many unsavory characters, at least a small percentage of whom might have been would-be robbers, pass me by without giving me so much as a second look.

For reasons that I am unlikely to discover, my complex was called "Mauritius Apartments." Their brochure (you got it from the leasing office, which was the only lavish structure in the entire complex) declared that Mauritius Apartments had apartments to suit every taste and every budget, that they had a happy family of tenants, that they had a caring, concerned management devoted to satisfying every need and every whim of its tenants. Needless to say, when my ice machine in the fridge was found to have a dangerous fungus growing in it, I found that the only thing the management was interested in was sitting in a comfy office reading People or Ella or Cosmopolitan. Calls from dissatisfied tenants were responded to with enthusiasm and courtesy, with many promises that the work would be done in no time at all—which was true: the work was done in "no time" in the sense that it was never done, and so there was never a time, or "no time" when it was done. OK. I am exaggerating. After several days of angry phone calls, a jovial handyman with a toothpick in his mouth finally showed up and decided to do something about the fact that all the ice cubes manufactured by my ice machine were grayish-green in color.

In my anxiety to escape from the office, I had not taken note of two things:

One, there was a car closely behind following me, which stopped just outside the parking lot of my complex. I mean, I'd seen this car but had failed to understand its connection to my future well-being.

And two, that there was somebody lurking in the shadows around the corner from my second-floor apartment. I saw this person for a second before he retreated into the shadows. Again, I failed to correctly appreciate the significance of this observation.

Instead, I rapidly got out of my car, cell phone to my ear, on hold for the Continental Airlines representative.

And then I climbed the stairs.

47

The sensation of being grabbed from behind is always unpleasant. I don't usually like to be dogmatic about anything, so let me rephrase: the sensation of being grabbed from behind is always unpleasant—*for me*. I'm sure somebody in the world thrives on this feeling; lovers like to do these kinds of things to each other, but as and when I have a full-time partner, I shall instruct him to lay off the grabbing-from-behind maneuver. From my point of view, this is a relationship-killer. The reason I bring this up is simple: when I reached the top of the stairs, when I inserted the key into my lock, and after I had opened the door, a human being rushed from behind, grabbed me, and pushed me on the floor. Ouch! As you can appreciate, this was not a lover's embrace, and it was most definitely painful. I was being beaten and perhaps was in the process of being killed. Naturally, I didn't get killed, or I wouldn't have been around to write about it. But I did get hurt. I fell directly on my nose, and even though the floor was carpeted, it felt as if someone had knocked me on the proboscis with a brick. My lip felt the impact as well, and after a sharp jab of pain, it went numb.

All I could see of the person on top of me were the wrists. They were a man's wrists. Was it George Zimaresh? But why? So far, he'd written letters. This seemed so different from his usual method of operation. But this was not the issue. The issue was that there was a man on top of me, my hands were below me, and I was gasping for air.

The face of this man came close to my ear, and I felt his hot breath as he whispered in a raspy tone, "Get out of Houston. Do it now, understand?"

I gasped in response: "If you'll get the hell off me, that's what I plan to do—immediately."

"Good," whispered the man. His voice sounded familiar—did I know him from somewhere? "I'm going to get off you, but if you turn around, I'll be forced to kill you."

That was what is referred to as a motivational speech. I lost all desire to see who my attacker was. I said, "Just get off. I can barely breathe. I won't try to look at you—promise."

I felt a sudden release of pressure.

I naturally refrained from looking at my attacker. I don't have an appetite for heroism, and I was past the stage of being curious. I was getting very clear signals that I wasn't wanted in Houston anymore. I intended to comply with my assailant to the fullest extent.

I was about to shift my body when a body—that is to say, somebody else's body—suddenly fell almost on top of me. Fortunately, I had moved slightly, and so it missed me by a few inches. I would certainly have been crushed had I not moved out of the way in time.

So whose body was this? And why had the apartment of Imogene Chaplin suddenly become the hot spot for falling bodies?

"Don't move, or I'll club you!" This voice came from behind me, and I was once again struck by how familiar it was. I didn't know if the voice was addressed to me or to the body of the fallen man, who was shielding his face with his hands so that I wouldn't see him.

I decided that the man, the man who said "Don't move" etc., wasn't talking to me. It was because I recognized the voice. It belonged to Dr. Hector Malone—remember him? My trainee in the dark art and science of forensic pathology.

48

Events were a clichéd blur, but not so blurry that I couldn't place the chap on the floor. I mean the man who had attacked me, threatened me to leave Houston, and so on. He was wearing a blue shirt and black pants, exactly like the guy who had dropped the letter off at the office, the letter warning me to get out of Houston. He'd decided to make his point even clearer by jumping on top of me. His face was shielded from me, and despite Hector prodding him with a baseball bat, he wouldn't reveal his face. But he didn't need to. I knew who he was.

"Roy—Dr. Culpepper!" I could barely believe it.

"This is Dr. Culpepper?" asked Hector, with shock in his voice.

"You know Dr. Culpepper?"

"I tried to get a job with his group," said Hector. "Before I applied for training with you guys."

It is a familiar story in the pathology world. Some people try to get jobs in lucrative private practices, don't make it, then change tracks and get some additional training.

Roy Culpepper was, by this time, slobbering and weeping. His whole body was shaking so violently that I was afraid that people in the apartment below me would soon begin complaining about the racket. The other day, I'd dropped a carton of bottled water, and it had scared the hell out of my downstairs neighbors. They'd jabbed repeatedly on the ceiling with a stick, that is to say, beneath my floor, to signal their disapproval of my actions.

"Jesus, shit, I'm sorry, Imogene. I didn't plan it to be this way." There was a long sob and a shudder. "I lost my mind. I was worried sick I'd said what I'd said to you. Then I thought you'd sue me for sexual harassment or something crazy like that. You see, I had to make sure you left Houston and never came back. Ohhhhhhhhhhhh!"

I nearly felt sorry for this man. Note the word *nearly*.

"What about the bit about being forced to kill me."

"I didn't mean that, Imogene, you've got to believe me. I—I—I—I couldn't hurt a fly."

"You hurt me pretty good."

"Jeez—I'm sorry. Shit. Am I going to go to prison?"

This brought forth a new volley of sobs. Additionally, he began to pound on the floor with his fists to further express his grief for ruining his life.

"Hey, Roy, do you mind? Sob all you want, but can you please cut out the fist-pounding?"

"Wha—" he asked, and then, as he understood, he made a low howling, whimpering sound. The man was a cornucopia of grief-stricken sounds. If I hadn't been so frightened, I would have felt sympathy for him.

But as it was, I felt little sympathy for him. I took Hector's cell phone and began dialing Helen Freud. This man deserved to be in jail.

I asked Hector why, or how, he had materialized so suddenly outside my apartment door.

"I followed you," he said. "Your secretary was worried about you."

"Oh, she was?"

"She said you sounded scared and a bit crazy—I'm only quoting her—but I think she meant that in a kind, motherly way."

"I'm not offended, Hector," I said.

"I wouldn't want to get her into trouble. I'm only clarifying my intent in following you. I'm not stalking you or anything."

"Understood," I said.

"I tried to stop you, but I couldn't. I even honked the horn."

"Oh, that was you?" I laughed. "I cursed you to damnation, not knowing what your problem was."

"You showed me the finger, actually, which was all right…under the circumstances."

"Thanks for understanding."

49

Freud was on the scene sooner than I expected. She was circling the area like a vulture in search of a suitable place to obtain nourishment. As she told me when she arrived, she was trying to decide between a Vietnamese soup and a burger from Wendy's. I felt that this information about her quest, though interesting, was neither relevant nor necessary, given the situation. My employer had attacked me from behind and had further threatened to kill me if I didn't do exactly as he ordered. I'm not saying I needed sympathy or understanding, but at the very least, I needed one repentant pathologist off my floor (and into jail, where he properly belonged).

Freud stared hard at Dr. Culpepper, who was at this time sitting on the floor in the lotus position, eyes closed and shaking his head. What was going through his mind? What one would expect at such a time, I imagine: he had just ruined his life from a socially viable point of view. He had committed sexual harassment followed by a physical assault on a female employee in an amazingly short period of time. He was also, I now saw, a very repulsive sort of man and pitiful in an odd sort of way. Like a monster. A monster who had just wrecked his own life and a monster who'd nearly wrecked my clavicle, which was hurting like mad.

"I'm going to have to ask you to stand up so I can cuff you," said Freud unemotionally.

He opened first the one eye and then the other. Then, in less time than it takes to tell, the man was flat on the ground, his face pressed against my shoes, and his hands tightly circling my ankles.

"Imogene, I beg you. Can you please forgive me? I'll be ruined. You understand, ruined."

I didn't care.

I asked him to please compose himself, to please let go of my ankles, and to please stop kissing my shoes. Such behavior was not dignified. "When you've screwed up your life," I said harshly, "you should at least accept it like a man."

"Oh Imogene, Imogene, Imogene, Imogene!" he wailed. This was beginning to turn into a scene from Shakespeare. So much so that Dr. Culpepper even proceeded to quote from Shakespeare. I would never have expected Shakespeare to come out of his mouth, but there it was: "The quality of mercy is not strained," he groaned, as his voice broke and changed pitch, "the quality of mercy is not strained. It droppeth as the gentle rain from heaven, you know. Mercy, mercy, for God's sake, Imogene, mercy!"

The man was plainly hysterical. Unfortunately for him, I felt totally unmerciful. I was angry. I did not feel sorry for him. I ignored his plea. I stood quietly as one of the other officers with Freud took him away in handcuffs.

And then Freud turned to me and dropped the bombshell.

"You okay now? I was just about to call you when you called me. I wanted to grab a bite before I went there. You see, the head's been found."

"What? Where? Whose head is it?"

She told me.

PART TWO: HEAD

50

Here's where Marion Best comes into the picture—again.

I can see you're shaking your head, asking yourself, who on earth is this Marion Best? That's the problem I face in keeping the story straight and not getting everyone, including myself, hopelessly muddled. But facts are like that. They come at you from all angles and are hard to keep straight. So, let me take a moment to refresh your memory about Mr. Marion Best.

We go back to an earlier time, which, of course, was not that long ago, earlier that morning, in fact. George Zimaresh had left his second letter to me on my desk at the scene of Dr. Felicity Moon's murder. He had ended the second letter with the following clue:

P.S. There is another clue you could pass on to the police (what can we do about the police? They are the ones who always get it wrong—at least in my books. But don't worry, I have faith in you). Here's the clue. It's a name. **Marion Best**.

Marion Best.

I remember how, at the time, we'd wondered about the name a bit, and Freud had decided to follow up on it. Her research unearthed quite a bit of information on Mr. Best. She didn't have a chance to share it with me. With all that was going on, she hadn't had a chance to do so. When bodies are piling up and pathologists are being attacked, there's a situation of information overload.

To declare it in just a simple sentence: Freud knew who Best was, what he did, what he had done, and what he *might have* done. Best was critical, critical to this whole saga.

In order to simplify matters, I'm going to take a slightly unconventional approach to storytelling and tell you about Mr. Best in a question-and-answer format. This way, we'll stick to the facts and keep the irrelevant crud out of the picture. As this is not a novel or a tale of lies, I think that it is okay to break the conventions of storytelling to make things a little less complicated.

So, first question: *Who was Marion Best?*

Answer: Marion Best was an actor.

Second question: *What kind of actor?*

Answer: Not a very successful one, or one who had seen slight success and wasn't seeing much of it lately (what some people unkindly refer to as "a *has-been* who has never really been"). In other words, he'd acted in some good parts in some good films (do you remember *The Underwear Romance?* In that movie, he played the part of the zucchini-obsessed psychiatrist, quite an important role). But then, the good parts died away. More recently, he'd been the window cleaner advising on the best way to remove ear wax in a commercial—understandably not the best role in his career. He almost struck gold a year ago when he was one of the finalists chosen to play the part of a famous personality in a made-for-TV series. *Which famous personality?* George Zimaresh. Zimaresh's life had been processed into a TV serial, about to start showing in less than a week. Marion Best had nearly been chosen to play the role of Zimaresh. Nearly. Somebody else beat him to it. (For the record, the shooting of this serial was completed, and in an effort to capitalize on Zimaresh's remarkable "death," the networks were speeding up to get it out sooner than they had planned.) In summary, Marion Best, like the majority of actors anywhere in the world, was basically mostly unemployed, scavenging for any part, no matter how small.

Next question: *What might he have done?*

Answer: Not clear. Killed someone, perhaps? Don't know.

Last question: *Where was he now?*

Answer: Not clear. In some other country, maybe? Don't know.

So there you have it. You now know what I knew then, as I was driven by Freud to the scene of the latest crime, or more precisely, the scene of the latest discovery, out in the outskirts of Houston, the north of Houston, close to the woods, where a human head had been discovered by a woman.

The name of the woman was Mrs. Marion Best.

51

A woman.

Marion Best's wife.

Mrs. Ingrid Best.

A little while ago, in an ice bucket with plenty of ice, she had found a human head. She heard a noise near the backdoor, like somebody throwing a pebble at a window, and went to investigate. There, she discovered the ice bucket, and she opened it, screamed and fainted, and, in general, displayed the kind of behavior of people when confronted with such a horrible sight. I guess the word horrible doesn't even do it justice. It is beyond horrible, and no one who has seen such a sight can ever describe it to another. I wish such a sight on nobody, but, as we all know, this is a difficult world, and our wishes often don't come true, and so, there it was—the head, Mrs. Ingrid Best, and her rather large neighbor, Mark, who hovered over her like a protective mother hen.

The word Ingrid, for some reason, always conjures up, inside my head, an image of a very tall, thin Swedish woman. Anyway, this Ingrid was in no way similar to the mental Ingrid who lives in my brain. No. This Ingrid was on the shorter side, slightly shorter than average, I would say, slightly dark, tanned, with a very pretty face; symmetrical, round, with a pretty mouth. Men always tell me that women are very inaccurate when it comes to telling who is pretty and who isn't. But this woman *was* pretty, and I bet that most men would find her so. Mark, her protector, certainly thought so. He gazed at her adoringly, like a sheepdog gazing at his master. The officers at the scene, too, were finding it difficult to keep their eyes off her.

Helen Freud, however, was not one of those officers and was, as she'd told me not too long ago, a devoted heterosexual. Her interest in Ingrid

Best was purely professional. She even managed to be kind and gentle, something I'd not seen in her before. In my own recent traumatic experiences, she'd been short on sympathy (but to be honest, she had toned down her usual macho behavior by appearing slightly bored and distant). But here, she was, like I said, incredibly gentle. It was almost as if she wanted to mother this pretty little woman.

"So what did you do, then?"

The woman sniffed. She wasn't actively weeping, but she was finding it hard to hold back her tears.

"I think I fell down."

"I found her," said Mark, slowly and heavily. He looked at me at this point with a hard, menacing look.

"Don't mind him," said Ingrid. "I think he likes you," she said to me and then added, as if addressing a child, "Don't you, Mark?"

Mark looked angrily at her and said nothing.

"Mark's my guardian angel. He looks scary, like Frankenstein, I know, but he's really sweet. He's a bit slow, as you can tell. He's got the mind of an eight-year-old. That's what Dr. Murtry told us, didn't he?" She rubbed his arm. "But we don't mind that, do we? Oh, I wish Marion would show up."

"We'll have to get to that in a minute, Mrs. Best. So you found her?" she addressed Mark. "What did you do?"

"I took it out," he answered, appearing surprised that anyone could ask such a strange, stupid question. Wasn't that the most obvious thing to do?

"I see. Why did you do that?" she asked Mark.

"I wanted to see whose head it was."

"I see. And whose head was it?"

"Mr. Zimaresh's. I know what Mr. Zimaresh looks like. He called me 'my boy.' He's not my dad," he said quickly, in case we drew the wrong conclusion.

"I know, Mark," said Freud softly. "How do you suppose Mr. Zimaresh's head got inside the ice bucket?"

Mark looked at her with bewilderment. "I can't tell everything. I'm only human. Somebody put him there, I'd say. That's how heads get inside ice buckets."

He said this with considerable feeling and without any trace of sarcasm.

Freud didn't respond. One has to make allowances for people with subnormal intelligence. It's not what he said but how he said it. He spoke slowly, with a vacant look in his eyes. That look spoke volumes.

"I'm on my own now," he said suddenly.

"What do you mean?"

"Marion wrote me that."

Ingrid sobbed.

"What do you mean wrote that?" Freud asked sharply.

"You don't know what wrote is?" Mark giggled.

Freud bit her lip. I imagine that had he been normal, she would have really given it to him. Instead, she simply said in a matter-of-fact way, "I know what *wrote* is, Mark. Did he leave you a note?"

"He did."

"What did the note say?"

"I can't remember the exact words. I think the words were: *Look after Ingrid.* Something like that."

"Where's the note?"

"I threw it in the trash can."

"Why? Wasn't that an important note to keep?"

Mark stared at her as if she'd just said the silliest thing he could imagine.

"I knew what it said. It said what it said. Why'd I need to keep it? It was trash. Nobody likes to keep trash."

"Right. Where did you throw it?"

"In the trash can, like I said."

"Why do you think he wrote that note?"

"Because he was going away."

"Where was he going?"

"I don't know. I can't tell everything. I'm only human."

That was the second time he said that. It wasn't a cocky, smart-ass comment he used to answer any question he couldn't answer. It seemed he used this phrase to answer life's complicated situations.

"Why would Mr. Best write such a note?" Freud asked Ingrid.

"How should I know? I was just his wife! He found more things to say to—to—Mark than to me!"

She plopped her face into her hands and shook, I think, with anger.

"Did you know he'd written this note?"

"Mark told me this morning."

"What did you do?"

"Beat the hell out of him. But he doesn't know where Marion is."

"Do you know where he is, Mark?" Freud persisted.

"No, I don't. He left me the note. I think he's disappeared. People just disappear sometimes, don't they? I can't tell everything. I'm only human."

He said it again.

"Okay. He left you a note. Where did you throw it?"

"I told you, in the trash can."

"Where was the trash can?"

"Where? At Mr. Zimaresh's house, of course."

52

For a few seconds, nobody spoke.

"Why were you at Mr. Zimaresh's house?"

"Marion said we had to go there."

"Did Marion say why?"

"He said we had a job to do."

"What was the job?"

Mark narrowed his eyes. He appeared to be thinking hard.

"I can't tell," he said. "I just went with Marion."

Freud said very slowly, as if she didn't want to be misunderstood. "Did Marion and you cut off Mr. Zimaresh's head?"

Ingrid stiffened. "You can't ask him those kinds of questions!" She yelled. "Marion wouldn't hurt a fly. This is crazy!"

She was close to shrieking.

"You don't have to answer this question," said Freud. "I'll just have to take you to the precinct."

"He has rights," Ingrid shot back. "Just because he looks like an adult doesn't mean he's one. He's got a problem! Can't you see? Are you blind? He's not like you and me. He's a child!"

Mark jumped up and moved very close to Freud.

"You do anything to her, and I'll break your legs," he said, clearly meaning it.

Freud didn't move and motioned her officers to stay back.

"You don't have to answer this question. We won't upset Mrs. Best. Is that okay?"

"That's better," he said, sounding pleased. "Marion said to look after Ingrid, and that's what I am gonna do." He paused. "She's right; Marion didn't hurt anybody, ever. I saw him with the earthworm. I wanted to step on him, but Marion said no. He took a stick and moved the earth-worm to the right. He saved that earthworm's life. Marion didn't cut off Mr. Zimaresh's head. That would be stupid." He paused again and said, "Mr. Zimaresh was very nice. He gave Marion some tea, and he gave me some cookies. With chocolate." He took a cookie out of his pocket as if this memory had suddenly sparked his desire to have a cookie as soon as possible. "Marion left me the note," he repeated.

"When was this? When did you go to Mr. Zimaresh's house?"

"Yesterday."

"What time?"

"I don't have a watch. It was the afternoon."

The head.

Naturally, this was the first thing I saw when we got there. I don't want to dwell on the subject. It was a head. He looked peaceful. Content. His eyes were closed. He was pretty well preserved for someone who'd been dead for nearly 24 hours in the Houston heat—the ice had done its job.

And I, who had seen many pictures of Zimaresh on the web recently, had no trouble recognizing him. It was him, all right. Zimaresh. Since this was his head, without a doubt, it was safe to conclude that he was really and truly dead and that somebody had done this to him, either with or without his participation. Finally, there was someone out there, maybe Marion Best, who'd done this to him. *With the help of a slow, mentally challenged giant with very large feet.*

53

I can imagine how those poor medieval folks felt when it finally became apparent that those apparently crazy scientists were right and that the world was not flat. I felt very similar. My whole theory had been based on a simple assumption: Zimaresh had killed someone else and had then performed a vanishing act. The only flaw with my hypothesis was that I was completely wrong. It was *Zimaresh* who was really dead, and *somebody else* had performed a vanishing act.

Helen Freud was in a moody, almost reflective state when we left the home of Marion Best.

"Don't you think you should've arrested him?"

"Who?"

"That guy, Mark?"

She sighed.

"Can't do that. I need proof. I know what you're thinking. I'm thinking the same. Zimaresh, who's clearly nuts, wanted to die in a bizarre way for all kinds of reasons. He wanted to sell more books, he wanted his daughter to sell more books, blah-blah-blah. Basically, the greedy bastard wanted more and more money, not just for himself but for his kids, his daughter. He felt that he'd been a bad guy, losing a whole bunch of money, and this was his way of making amends. I can understand that. He knew he was going to die anyway because of the cancer in his brain. So he plotted his own death and got Marion Best and this giant to help him. This would explain the two pairs of footprints we found at the scene, one normal size, one very big. You noticed, didn't you, the very large feet on Mark? Well, so they did it, and Marion ran away, understandably, leaving the simple friend to take care of Mrs. Marion." She paused to take a deep breath. "But now, we run into a problem. The problem is very simple.

You and I were there when the door was opened. You and I were there when we entered the room. And you and I were there when you and I saw that, with the exception of Mr. Zimaresh, who was missing his head, there was nobody else in that room. If you have Marion Best and his big buddy, where did they go? How did they vanish? Can you imagine the D.A. going before a jury trying to explain that? No. This is an impossible crime. Until I can figure out a way of explaining how it was done, I can't arrest anyone, especially not someone with subnormal intelligence. I don't want the whole world shouting out police brutality and calling me a bitch."

"Well, and that's my point exactly," I argued. She'd summed up the points accurately. "Why can't you call him in and ask him how they did it? He can tell you how the impossible was done."

Freud snorted. The woman, as I've previously noted, was an accomplished snorter. With one snort, she could communicate more than someone else could have with a long, passionately argued speech. With one snort, she told me that I was certifiably insane for having made such a foolish suggestion.

"You think that this poor fellow can tell us how they pulled off a stunt that is impossible for ALL of us to figure out?"

"Why not? He was there."

"He was there. But only to help out—like a soldier ant. You think he has any freaking idea how they did it just because he was there? And, by the way, we have no proof he was there. We have the footprints, and we'll have to do a search and find shoes and all that—we'll have to do that very soon—like immediately. But we need warrants for that, as you know. I know I've got to call him in for questioning. But not at this moment. I've got to think about it. Formulate a hypothesis. At the very least, I've got to question other suspects. His daughter, his heirs, his business associates, anyone who had a good reason to get rid of Papa Zimaresh, and I believe all of them did. I've got to discuss with my chief and with the D.A. This is a complicated crime. I'm not about to book somebody like Mark. If he'd been a normal guy, I'd have no problem. But you see, I can't. I just can't. Got to think about it first. I'm not an impulsive girl."

I looked at her, and for the first time, I saw that I had judged her wrong. She was not simply a macho, boisterous, jump-headlong-into-a-crisis kind of person. She was, even though it was hard to imagine, the kind who thought things through. Not impulsive, as she said.

54

In summary, I didn't quit Houston and leave. Instead, I headed back to my office—I mean Alec's office—and almost immediately received a phone call from my father.

"M'dear, I've been exercising the little grey cells," he said. "This case of yours is quite fascinating. You know the allusion, don't you, m'dear?"

"What allusion?" I was distracted by a bee buzzing against the window of the office.

"The allusion to the little grey cells; Agatha Christie's detective Hercule Poirot used that phrase constantly."

"Yes, Dad," I said a bit wearily. I like talking to my father; he generally has an unusual point of view to offer, but right at that moment, I just felt tired and wanted to sit quietly and sip some herbal tea.

"Anyway, I began to think of your case and detective stories because, you see, I remembered something. It suddenly occurred to me that I'd read somewhere about a case similar to yours. About a missing head. A very peculiar case, nearly as puzzling as yours."

"Really?" I felt a stirring of interest.

"Yes, m'dear. A case—fiction, of course—and I scratched my head for nearly an hour before I remembered—G.K. Chesterton. Remember G.K. Chesterton?"

"Vaguely."

"Tut-tut, m'dear, what's happening to you? When you're over this crisis, I'll try to re-educate you about the finer things in life. Chesterton is one of them. But that is not the point. What was I saying? Oh yes, the missing head business. Chestertown created the famous priest detective, Father Brown. Jog your brain cells, m'dear. Father Brown, a brilliant character, able to solve the most extraordinarily difficult crimes with the minimum of effort. Excuse me, m'dear, while I attend to this tickle in my nose." There was the sound of a hearty sneeze, followed by a sniff. "Most gratifying. I sometimes think that a good sneeze can be the best tonic for low spirits. I generally feel awake and vibrant post-sneeze. But where was I? Oh yes, Chesterton and Father Brown. In one of his cases, Father Brown solves a seemingly impossible crime. A man is found murdered in a garden from which no one can escape, but the funny thing is that the man is missing a head. Oh, and there was no weapon either, much like in your case. I dare say your Mr. Zimaresh drew his inspiration from Chesterton."

"But what was the solution?" I asked desperately. My father has the most maddening way of jumping all over a topic, coming to a conclusion when you least expect it.

"The solution? Oh, Father Brown, who was one of the guests at the party, solved the crime without any problem. The murderer tossed the head over the high wall of the garden, and the weapon had been removed from the scene, which neatly accounted for the missing head and the missing weapon. Now, what do you think of that?"

"Dad," I said, with a touch of exasperation—I will not hide this fact. "Dad, it is quite obvious to all of us here that the head and the weapon were removed from the scene. This accounts for why they weren't there. Our problem is that there was a heavy door, and our problem is that the heavy door was locked, and nobody could've tossed anything larger than an ant anywhere. It's a different problem altogether. It's possible that Zimaresh or the murderer got the idea from Chesterton, but this is an *impossible* murder. A head and a weapon don't just vanish from a room."

"But don't you see, that is my precise point! A head and a weapon don't just vanish from a room, like you say. So, the conclusion is that they were taken out, and you haven't quite figured out how. That's all you have to do."

"Thanks, Dad," I said glumly. *Thanks for stating the obvious.*

"Cheer up, ducky. I know you're disappointed with your old man. I used to have the same sort of problem with my father. He kept telling me things I thought I already knew. But I didn't know them. Nobody knows everything, and sometimes we don't even know the things we think we know. Sometimes, what we need is a fresh point of view. M'dear, I'm about to offer you a fresh point of view."

"What is it?" I asked.

"I have a friend who just happens to be passing through Houston. He's an American, as it turns out, a very accomplished one. He's a psychologist."

"I don't need a psychologist."

"This guy you need. All I'm saying is he might be very helpful to you. Let me ask you a question: you were there when they opened the door. Are you sure you saw everything there was to see?"

"What do you mean?"

"You didn't see the murderer with the head in a bag and carrying a very large weapon?"

"No, Dad, clearly I didn't, otherwise we wouldn't be having this conversation."

"Listen, child, it's very simple. You saw something important. You just don't know what it is. That's where my friend might come to your assistance. He can talk to you and help you put the whole case in perspective. He can make you remember and focus on something that you saw that you think you didn't see. People didn't spot the gorilla, did they?"

"What gorilla?"

"Something he told me about. A man dressed in a gorilla suit walked through a room, and nobody saw him."

"But that's impossible!"

"Yes, but absolutely true. Nobody was expecting a gorilla to walk past them, so nobody saw the gorilla. You can talk to him about it. Let me give you his name and telephone number. Ready with the pen, m'dear?...His name is Seldon Fitzpur."

55

The talk with my father set me thinking about G. K. Chesterton and the missing head story. Yes, Zimaresh had most likely drawn his inspiration from Chesterton. What a tantalizing premise! A head disappears in a situation where a head couldn't have disappeared. That Zimaresh was familiar with Chesterton and his detective was proved by the fact that the book you had to remove to get to the secret passageway from his study was none other than Chesterton's *The Complete Father Brown*. It could've just been a coincidence—but I believed otherwise.

Turning to the other subject, the gorilla—

Notwithstanding the gorilla (was it really true? Or just an urban legend?), I didn't seriously think I was going to meet Mr. Fitzpur and get him to help me with my problem. But I was wrong. Life takes a pattern that is different from what we conceive.

No sooner had I hung up the phone than I was informed that somebody was waiting to speak to me.

The day had gone too long. Already, it was late evening, and we were still here. Rebecca had decided to stay, well past her time, to help out. I saw concern in her eyes, as well as suspicion that I might crack up any minute and do something crazy. She kept passing my—I mean Alec's—office, carrying this or that, but in reality, to keep an eye on me.

I sighed. I longed for a quiet moment. You know the feeling? You just want to chill out and not see anyone for just a little bit, and then you get recharged in some mysterious way until you feel the desire to socialize again. And then you socialize. But I'd been socializing with humans in good and bad ways almost constantly for the last 24 hours, with only a few hours of sleep. I think I'd socialized enough for a month or two. I needed time off. But such was not to be.

Ray Marsh—for such was this chap's name—was probably no older than twenty-five (or so it seemed; he was, as I later found out on the internet, forty-two and obscenely young-looking). He was tall, clean-shaven, with messy hair tied neatly into a ponytail, no doubt some kind of trendy hairstyle. Everything about him was expensive: his pants, the colorful striped shirt, the leather jacket (for which there was no need since it was so bloody hot), his shoes, and his sunglasses (which he removed).

As he informed me, he was the director of the TV serial based on Zimaresh's life: The Wonder Murder Boy of Houston. He was here to tell me something. Something important. Why me and not the police? I wanted to know. I asked him.

"I've been following this story. You seem connected with him—he keeps writing you letters."

I shook my head wearily. I couldn't explain everything to the whole world. But I couldn't stop explaining, either. I said,

"You're under an illusion. Mr. Zimaresh had a weird sense of humor—no, humor is not the word since he's dead, and death is not a fitting subject for humor—but he certainly had a weird sense of the way things ought to be. He picked me out—I have no shame in admitting it—because I am so new to this business, so inexperienced, so *inept*." I emphasized this word. "He thought it would be more fun—or interesting—to have a complete novice handle the case, and so he made a few discreet inquiries, found when I was on call, and my colleagues were out of town, and planned his demise to coincide with my on-call night. The only *connection* we had, Mr. Marsh, is that Mr. Zimaresh had such a low opinion of my intellect. He needed someone to make a thorough mess of the whole forensic aspect of it. It makes the story more interesting, doesn't it? Stupid Forensic Pathologist Completely Botches Up Forensic Investigation. He's sent letters to the press, so the press remains enlightened about the whole affair and can keep tabs on my incompetence."

Ray Marsh was looking at me in an interested sort of way, in an almost whimsical manner, much in the same way as he would regard an interesting mental patient exhibiting a high degree of non-violent psychosis. He even smiled slightly.

"I don't know how bright you are," he said, "Since we hardly know each other. But I think you've judged the situation correctly. I was curious to see you. My producer—the network, actually—wants to expand the show—we're going to add a few episodes. The murder's got to be in, and this means that you've got to be in."

"When you say *in*, what precisely do you mean?"

"We need to have someone play Dr. Chaplin—play you, in the movie—an actress. But speaking to you, I'm having a creative breakthrough. An idea. You see, Dr. Chaplin, a director is like a net. Any interesting idea and the director's brain goes buzzing. Can I tell you my idea?"

"I have a suspicion you're going to tell me."

He looked at me vacantly and then suddenly smiled.

"I think you yourself should play you in the movie. That would be a great angle from the marketing perspective. You're already national—I should say international—news."

"International?"

"You've been mentioned by name in India, Japan, Malaysia, China, and Finland, and this is only a partial list."

I took a deep breath. I don't know everybody in the world (thank God). So why would I care? It wouldn't matter what some Finnish person thought about me. Even so, I didn't appreciate being thought of as a colossal fool on an international level.

"Mr. Marsh, I don't think I can act—"

"You're perfect for the part—look at it this way: you need no acting to be you. Just come on the set, be yourself, go home, make a ton of money."

I saw his point. It was seductive, this business about a ton of money.

"I'll have to think about it," I said, meaning it. Pathology, as a career, wasn't panning out the way I wanted it to. Now that I'd sent my boss to jail, who would be willing to hire me? Even though it was that stupid, horny Culpepper's fault, people wouldn't see things that way. All anybody would think of is "that girl who got mixed up in the headless murder case and got into trouble with her boss." People don't bother to go into details. They don't look deep enough. It's enough that I was unlucky enough to be mixed up in something bad. It hardly mattered that none of it was my fault. I hadn't chosen to get a suicidal writer interested in me, just as I hadn't chosen to drive my married employer crazy with love or lust for me.

"What's there to think about? But take your time; how about I call you tomorrow?"

"Tomorrow sounds good. I'll call you tomorrow," I said. I was in a sort of a daze. Most people don't get a chance to be TV stars. I couldn't ignore this offer merely on the grounds that I couldn't act.

"May I ask you a question?" I asked.

"Shoot," he said.

"Did you know Marion Best?"

56

"Unlucky bastard," said Marsh.

"In what way?"

"He was the best man for the job, in my opinion. But Zimaresh didn't like him. I thought the guy probably deserved a break—considering he fit the part so perfectly. I am not a humanitarian when it comes to work. I make movies for TV, and that is serious business. A lot of money goes into these projects, and if you don't do well, you don't get to make any more movies. It's that simple. There's only one requirement to make it in show business. You've got to succeed. I've got to look at the bottom line. I'm just telling you this so you know where I'm coming from. But in this case, I felt sorry for the poor loser. From what he told me, he barely had enough to make his house payments. He was doing this ad and that ad for some local sponsors in Houston, but you know how much those people pay. Next to nothing. Actors have a tough life. Playing parts seems like a nice way to make money. Somebody dresses up as a priest or a cop or a prime minister, and what could be an easier way to make money? Unfortunately, everyone wants to do this, and very few people are really good enough to do it well. Most actors don't make any money doing it. Like Marion. I thought he ought to do it and that he'd be good in the role. But Zimaresh had veto power over who got to play him. He picked Jim, who's good, don't get me wrong, but I think Marion would've done it better. But Marion didn't get to do it because of Zimaresh," he repeated.

"Why do you think Mr. Zimaresh didn't want Marion to do the role?"

"I don't know. He was a weird guy, I mean Zimaresh—very interesting from the entertainment point of view, but I felt uneasy with him. Maybe he was having a bad day. I don't know. I think he felt bad about it afterward."

"Why do you say that?"

"Well, I saw the two of them having lunch. Which was very strange since I saw them having lunch in L.A., and Marion is down in Houston. He must have come up for lunch with Zimaresh, or maybe he was there for a part…I don't know. George gave him a packet. You know what I thought was in the packet?" He stopped as he widened his eyes to convey a look of extreme significance. "I thought there was money in the packet. It looked like a fat bundle of cash. That's why I say George probably felt bad. He decided to dish out some dough, quite a bit of dough judging from the size of that packet."

I took a deep breath.

"Can you be absolutely sure he was giving money to Mr. Best?"

He clicked his tongue irritably. "No, of course, I can't. I didn't see him waving dollar bills in the air, if that's what you mean. The packet looked like it had money inside it. It was one of those brown envelopes, you know, an 8 by 11. I can't swear that there was money inside, but I am pretty sure there was."

So that was that.

"I think you need to talk to someone," I said.

57

It seemed logical then to put forward the following hypothesis, which I scribbled on my notepad (if it sounds repetitious, it is. I was faced with facts that made no sense. I thought that by writing it out, it might make more sense. But it didn't).

Here's what I wrote:

George Zimaresh was dying. He needed to fix his finances to leave his heirs comfortably off. How to go about it? Plan a magnificent murder. He had a TV movie or serial, a new book, a daughter who was writing a new book. All he needed was the buzz to bring the millions home. He chose someone who might be willing to carry out his plan. Somebody who needed cash. Like Marion Best, especially since Zimaresh had prevented Marion from getting a good job—playing Zimaresh! He got Marion out to L.A. for some reason, maybe because L.A. is not Houston. He gave him the blood money, witnessed by Ray Marsh. And then he put the impossible murder into action. Marion got help from Mark and left him a note asking him to take care of his wife. Does Mrs. Best know about all this? Is she planning to meet him somewhere, in some other country? Don't know. But no doubt Freud will be checking all these possibilities herself.

This, then, was a snapshot of the way my cerebral cortex was seeing the pattern. The biggest unknown, of course, was how he had managed to pull it off. How do you decapitate someone and then disappear from the locked room, together with the head, a giant assistant, and the weapon, without anybody seeing them? I was there and hadn't seen anything. Or had I missed something like my father insisted?

I kept repeating these thoughts: *impossible…I was there…didn't see any-thing…or did I?* etc., etc. These ideas kept banging off the walls of my skull like pointless mantras.

I must have been in a rather suggestible state. Or else I wanted to get away from it all for a little while. Or it may have been a combination of both of these factors. A tired brain needing a change, something different. Because I did something, something that I didn't think I would do.

58

Mr. Fitzpur agreed to see me immediately. He was staying at the Marriott Medical Center, just a short hop from where I was.

"I know your Dad well," he told me when I arrived at his hotel room. "I think you may find this helpful."

He seated me on the large sofa and then took his own seat at a curious angle, to the side and slightly to the back, so that I had to turn my head back to see him and talk to him. I thought this was an uncomfortable way of carrying on a conversation, but as I was to find out, he had done this for a reason.

He served me a chamomile tea. I don't know about you, but chamomile doesn't taste like I expect tea to taste. But I have to admit it's soothing. I was soon in a very relaxed frame of mind.

Seldon Fitzpur, once I got over the fact that anybody could really have a name like that, was a perfectly average-looking old man. He must've been nearly eighty. He was small, thin, and was hardly the sort of man you'd give a second look to. The best way of describing him would be to say that here was a man who wasn't good-looking or ugly or distinguished in any way. Being with him was like being with no one in particular. It was almost like being inside a bus next to an old guy you don't really notice or think about in any way. In a way, he was like my father. A kind old man but otherwise completely ordinary.

He did say some interesting things, however.

"Let me give you a bit of background," he said. "I'd like to begin with the gorilla."

(See what I mean? Thought-provoking stuff.)

"A researcher did a study on what is known as inattentional blindness. Have you heard of that? It's the kind of blindness that happens when you're not paying attention. Let's say a man walks into this room, dressed up as a gorilla, and thumps his chest. Will you notice him?"

"I guess he'd be hard to miss."

"Perfect response. Very logical. A man disguised as a chest-thumping gorilla can't just walk into a room and blend into the furniture. Or so we would like to think. But in fact, this researcher proved the opposite. He had several thousands of students watch a video of two teams playing basketball. The students had to keep their attention on the ball. Then, a short while into the video, a man wearing a gorilla costume came into the room in the middle of the screen, thumped his chest, and left. Do you know how many of the thousands of students watching this video saw this gorilla?"

I waited for him to tell me.

"Half. Of the several thousands of people he tested, nearly half didn't even see the gorilla. Can you imagine? Thousands of people saw a tape with a man dressed up as a gorilla thumping his chest in the middle of a basketball court, and they never saw the gorilla! How is that possible, you ask? Are you asking this, by the way?"

You can bet I was asking this. This stuff was hard to believe.

"Did this really happen?"

"It really did happen. But I am glad you ask. Because you see, many of those who didn't see the gorilla got very upset. They claimed that the tape they'd seen didn't have any gorillas. The reason why they did that (which is also the reason why you had to ask if this really happened) is the same: It is pretty unbelievable. If a gorilla came and sat next to you, you would be sure to notice, wouldn't you?"

"Of course."

"Unless you were focusing on something else. So, let us suppose if you were really staring hard at something else, you might miss this gorilla. Possible?"

"I suppose, but I have to say that I am skeptical."

"Please say hello to our friend," he said suddenly.

"What friend?" It was then that I realized that I wasn't the only person sitting on the sofa. Next to me was someone in a gorilla suit. I jumped.

"When, how?" I babbled, sounding only slightly more intelligent than an average gorilla.

"This is Mrs. Fitzpur, Emily, who helps me with this demonstration. I noticed you were a bit puzzled by the way I was sitting. It made you turn your head, caused you some discomfort, I think, but you had to keep looking at me to remain polite. So you didn't see Emily come in and take a seat next to you. Dressed as a gorilla, naturally. Just to prove a point. This is a less dramatic demo than the one with the gorilla in the tape, but this is more personal, in my opinion. It brings the point home. I know it's not the same thing as the invisible gorilla experiment—but you see what I mean."

"How long have you been sitting here?" I asked, my heart rate returning closer to normal.

"A few minutes, my dear," she said in a thin voice.

Mrs. Fitzpur, Emily, took off the gorilla's head to reveal an elderly woman with silvery gray hair, a wrinkled but pretty face, and nearly colorless eyes—I mean pupils that were almost transparent, a little gray maybe. Emily took my hand in her large gorilla hand and shook it.

"Don't mind Sellie, sweetheart. He likes to put on a show. It's always been a problem with him. He likes to show everyone how wrong they are."

"I don't mind at all," I said, feeling strangely invigorated. A sweet old lady dressed as a gorilla on a sofa next to me, and I didn't even notice. Well, well. Now, what exactly had gone on in Zimaresh's study the night we broke into it? What hadn't I seen?

59

"Inattentional blindness," he said. "I think it should be called *attentional* blindness: you are focusing so hard on something else that you miss out on what is really important. Let me ask you, what is really important to you?"

"What is really important," I replied, "Is how the killer managed to escape from a locked room without being seen, with a head and weapon in tow. They had to get out somehow, and they did, but we can't even begin to understand how. The police have checked the door. The lock was rock solid, no hanky panky about it. It couldn't have been fidgeted with or locked from the outside somehow, using magnets or any such stuff. There were secret passageways, but one of them was a blind loop. The other was a tunnel under the room connected by a fake tree large enough to hide a man inside the room and one on the outside of the room—but the way the trees were designed, the door leading out of the trees could only be locked from *inside* the tree. But the one that was *outside* the room was *locked,* and the one *inside* the room was the one that was *unlocked,* which could only mean that nobody had left the room using the tree route. Instead, somebody may have entered the room by way of the trees. So, how did they leave the room? That's the only question, really."

"Exactly. Keep saying that to yourself because that is the only way you'll figure it out. You want to figure it out, don't you?"

He looked at me with a blank yet inviting expression in his eyes.

"Yes, I want to figure it out," I said. "But it seems so, so, difficult. The place was crawling with police officers. You see, Mr. Zimaresh or the murderer, whoever planned it, went out of his way to attract attention. He—or it could be a she—made sure that there would be plenty of police officers. There were numerous 911 calls. Calls were also made to individual police officers using a private line from inside the study—prob-ably Zimaresh made those calls. The result was that the place was full of police officers. They were like ants. For anybody to escape with so many cops—well, it's simply unbelievable."

"Why do you think he—or she—wanted to have so many police officers there?"

"To make it seem even more impossible. Whoever planned this was so sure of not getting caught that he made it all the more difficult. Have you seen the news? One reporter is calling it 'The impossible murder of headless in Houston.' Everyone is making a big deal of the fact that there were so many cops who barged into a room that had just been broken into. And there was nobody there. No one but a headless victim. 'Houston's vanishing murderer' is how the Houston Daily calls it."

"But you know what you've said can't be true," chuckled Fitzpur. "People don't just vanish into thin air. There had to be someone in the room, and that person had to leave somehow. That is what you have to focus on. This is what has interested me about this case from the very beginning. This is why I am here," he said, "I asked your father to put me in touch with you. You were there, and so you must have seen something, even if you don't realize it. I think I can help you recover that memory, even if you aren't aware that you have any such memory. Our minds see and hear more than we know about."

Yeah, yeah! I thought. He sounded like a page from a self-help book.

"I can see that you are doubtful. I just read a popular book called *Blink*. It's very interesting. It is full of information about how our brains process information. All kinds of information, in split seconds, without our even being aware of it. So, one can see without actually seeing—or being aware that one has seen something. I'm almost sure that you saw something. I think I can help you remember what you saw. Would you like to undertake a test?"

What could I do but agree? As long as it didn't involve taking hallu-cinogens or running around the room lighting incense, I was game.

60

The test was actually quite simple.

First, he made me tell him the whole story. From the start.

"This is to help you focus on the issue. To get your subconscious mind ready, in the mood, so to speak."

I was all for my subconscious mind to get into the mood. I told him as briefly as I could. The scene; the victim minus the head; the letter to me; the blood, the copious amount of blood; the passageway leading to the room where the murder had actually taken place; two sets of footprints, one small, one large; how we later found out the blood was from a camel, stolen from the new private Zoo at Houston, where Zimaresh had managed to position himself on the board of directors; the business of the two large fake trees—the inside one and the outside one, and how the inside one was unlocked while the outside one was locked, etcetera, how the tree doors could only be locked from inside (exasperating, isn't it, that all the important doors we were running into could only be locked from the inside?

I went over the subsequent murder of Felicity Moon by Spriggs and Spriggs's murder by someone else, probably Best; the discovery of the head, the tall giant simple fellow with very large feet. I went over my belief that Zimaresh was behind it all since who else could've gotten the camel blood? It was too much of a coincidence that somebody else had planned it. I asserted that even though Zimaresh's head was now in the cooler at the morgue, it changed very little. It just meant that like he'd "said" from the beginning, he had orchestrated his own demise, with instructions to his killer to make his head surface a little later, all for a cause that seemed good to him: more money for those he left behind—his daughter in particular. It made perfect sense, even if he couldn't be around to reap the benefits.

Lastly, I told him about Marion Best and the fact that Best left a mysterious note to his rather big, not very bright neighbor asking him to look after the pretty Ingrid Best, the woman who discovered Zimaresh's head. I made a big play out of the fact that Best and the giant were at Zimaresh's house yesterday, on the day of the party. That could only mean that Best and Mark did the head number on Zimaresh, after which Best vanished, knowing full well that the simple giant was too simple to ever pay for the crime—or even be able to tell the cops how it was done. You didn't have to be a psychiatrist to appreciate that Mark, Best's neighbor, was very slow, probably with a very low IQ, and completely unable to execute a crime of this magnitude on his own or ever be convicted for it. "Ray Marsh, the guy making the movie of Zimaresh's life, saw Zimaresh handing over what looked like a fat packet of money to Best," I told Dr. Fitzpur. As far as I was concerned, this sealed the whole affair. Zimaresh had paid Best to do what he did. Now, all that remained was the unsolvable portion of the crime. How had Best and Mark disappeared from the scene of the crime?

Fitzpur seemed to be lost in thought, and for some moments, I wondered if the old man had had a stroke or something. He was so silent and so distant that he was unreachable. After a minute or so of silence, I wondered if I should jab or poke him in the arm to confirm that he was still conscious, but then unexpectedly, his mouth began to move, and words began to come out of his mouth as if he'd just woken from a dream.

"I see. Very clever amusement," he said. "Amusement, of course, from a perverted point of view. Mr. Zimaresh is a mystery writer—a good mystery writer?" he asked.

"Not really. I've read a couple of books by him. He's average—well, actually, I don't remember."

"I would've read some more books by him just to get an idea of the way his mind works. But never mind. The point is that it seems, from all that you've said, that this was planned by Zimaresh. He's a mystery writer. OK. What do mystery writers do? They create illusions. That's all. They present the truth in a skewed way, hoping to make readers think in a *particular* way. What I mean is that they make the readers focus on all the wrong issues so that readers ignore what is really important in the context of the story. In other words, mystery writers make use of attentional or inattentional blindness. They make you pay attention to nonsense so that you miss out on the sense. Bad mystery writers never reveal the essential clues, of course, but I think in this case, Mr. Zimaresh didn't really have an opportunity to hide too many essential clues (even if he may have wanted to). Therefore, you open the door, the door that could only have been locked from inside, and you go inside. Once inside, you see what there is—nothing appears to be hidden, but something has to be hidden obviously: A man, maybe two men, a weapon, a head. So he's had to play with your minds. Somehow, he distracted your attention, so you didn't see what was really important."

I shook my head so violently that there may have been a real risk of causing brain damage.

"Impossible. I was there. I saw what was there and what wasn't there. What *wasn't* there was a man, maybe two men, a weapon, and a head. I'm absolutely convinced."

"Let's see if I can un-convince you. You're going to play back that entire scene in your mind. OK? To begin, I'm going to dim the lights. Just breathe gently for a few minutes, please."

I did as he asked. I think more than a few minutes must have passed because I felt bored—bored but relaxed, I should say. Not bored and anxious. You know what I mean? You're bored, and you're anxious as hell to stop the feeling of boredom; you want to run around the room, stroke a wild dog, do anything to end the boredom. This was not like that.

I was fairly bored but fairly content at the same time. As I said, relaxed. The room was quiet, the sofa was comfortable, and my mind felt at ease. I yawned.

"Now think about the problem," he said. I thought he had left the room. He may have done so and then come back inside. I smiled at him sheepishly.

"You have just opened the door, and you have just gone inside. Don't try to remember. Just put yourself there, back in the room, seeing what you saw. Don't try to force it. Just see whatever you are seeing. Are you seeing what's inside?"

"Yes," I said.

"Tell me what you see."

What I saw were images, like little snapshots. It's not at all like in a movie, you know, we don't remember like that. The past doesn't come back neatly like a continuous movie scene, with things happening one after the other. Instead, the mind sees something like a montage or a collection of images coming fast, fast, one after the other. That was what I saw. I wasn't forcing it. I was just there, and the scene was unfolding in choppy little pieces.

Fitzpur taped what I said while in that relaxed, trance-like state. He made me listen to it afterward. I copied it down later. Here's some of what I told him:

61

"I see the man…no head. There's blood. All over the freaking place. Tons of police officers. Forget about keeping the scene intact. They're all over the room, looking wildly like mad dogs. But there's no one there. There's the tree, the inside tree, and the inside tree-door is shut. From where I stand, I can see the smooth contour of the tree, and so I am sure the tree-door is shut. People are looking confused. I am confused. Helen is shaking her head; it makes no sense.

"It is pretty horrible, which sounds like an understatement. A man without a head is a very ugly, frightening sight. I feel a little sick and scared and, of course, terrified because, at the base of it, we all fear for our own lives, and seeing someone dead like that is an awful reminder of our own mortality. What is so damn amazing is that we've just opened the door, the place is full of cops, and the crazies who did this are not here. Surely, if the killers were still here, we'd see them. Apart from myself, Simon, and the victim, everybody else in the room (and there's a ton of people) is either a uniformed officer or a cop-out of uniform, like Helen Freud and a couple of her assistants. But even with all these people, we don't see him. I am baffled. Helen's baffled, too. She snorts.

"I see the clues. They make no sense. What's the big deal with the trees? Why have all these cops, unless it is to deliberately draw attention to how impossible the crime is? Imagine—every cop and his mother are here, and the killers disappear from under our noses!

"We need the help of Perkins. He comes obediently. Perkins is a proper fellow. Nothing can ruffle him, it seems. He comes in very elegantly, putting his foot over the police tape. He walks in, very dignified. He trips over something—the police tape, maybe? Anyway, he gets his hair out of shape, rather like Bob Hope in an old movie I saw once. He looks very comical, such a very proper man, looking as if he'd been in a typhoon. I guess he doesn't apply gel to his hair, which is why his hair got all out of shape. Anyhow, a moment later, I see that he looks baffled. Or surprised. It is hard to read his face. I catch his eye, and he smiles politely and runs his hand over his head, slowly bringing it back in line. I remember thinking, isn't he supposed to have gel in his hair or something to keep it down? I guess the image I have of valets or butlers is from movies—and they all seem to have their hair greased down and wax-like. Not Perkins, though.

"We go to the tree inside the room. The inside tree door is open. This means that somebody came into the room through here because the tree door can only be locked from the inside. The outside tree door is locked, which means nobody left through this pathway—if somebody'd gone that way, the outside tree door would've been open—since it can only be locked from the inside. *So somebody came into the room from the outside using the tree route.* Who? The killer? Perhaps. But why didn't he leave through the inside tree, as any logical, reasonable person would have? Obviously, to make this into an *impossible* murder. Whoever did this didn't leave through the inside tree door."

I wonder if you noticed it. But there were a couple of clues in here, one of which I totally missed, again, but the other was fairly straightforward, even though it occurred to me in the car when I was driving back. I simply had to call Helen. Let me explain:

62

So I was standing there again. And the room was almost exactly as messy as it was the last time I had seen it. The blood had been mopped up, it is true, but otherwise, it had stayed the same. This was a crime scene, and so the area of Zimaresh's study remained barred to entry by police tape. Given the nature of the crime, Helen had decided to post a police officer there around the clock. Thus, no one—and I mean no one—unless it was a cop—or somebody from the forensic side—had entered this room in the last twenty-four or more hours since Zimaresh's body had been discovered.

The door. I have mentioned the door before. The door of the study. A sturdy structure, completely impenetrable. Experts had been through the door, in a manner of speaking. They had studied it, contacted the manufacturer, examined the lock, and had come to the inevitable conclusion. It was truly impossible to lock the room from the outside. There was no key to the door. The way one locked it from the inside was to turn three levers, each of which slid a solid steel bar into one of three holes in the door frame. Once these locks were turned, nothing—and I mean nothing—could have opened the door from the outside. A magnet, no matter how strong, applied to the outside of the door would have been useless. Stainless steel doesn't give a flip for magnets—or at least that's what I've been told. Bottom line: The door had been locked from the inside, and there was no way around it.

But the fake trees were the subject of our present visit. The trees were exactly as we'd left them. That is to say, the inside tree door was open, and the outside tree door was locked, leading to the other inevitable conclusion, which I will repeat, at the risk of sounding maddeningly repetitious: Not only had somebody not left the room using the tree route, but somebody may have actually come into the room using this route. But this wasn't the only conclusion: the possibility remained that *no one* had used that route at all that night. The way the trees were designed, at any given time, *one of the doors had to remain open at any given time*—unless somebody was in the tunnel between them and had locked both tree doors from the inside.

"Helen, I may be nuts, but I remembered it clearly while I was in that trance or whatever," I told her. Helen Freud's expression told me that she had a deep distrust of trances or any other foo-foo psychic states. She liked objective facts. And objective facts didn't require you to enter knee-deep into a meditative trance. From her point of view, the story became suspect when a clinical psychologist-cum-philosopher told you about invisible gorillas, gave you chamomile tea, and asked you to take deep breaths. But she heard me out.

This is what I told her:

"I remember, as clear as a bell, that I saw from the corner of my eye, from where I stood after I entered the room, that the inside tree door was closed—or locked when we came into the room for the first time. The contour was smooth."

What I meant was that if the door was locked, it was flush with the tree, and you couldn't see the edge of the door jutting slightly beyond the circumference of the tree trunk. But when the door was open, the contour of the trunk was no longer smooth because you could see the edge of the tree poking outwards. This was the way we were seeing it then.

I was there doing a test. I was standing roughly where I remembered standing when I was in the room when I first entered the room. Helen was standing right next to me (that is to say, at this time, she was standing next to me; the last time we'd been inside the room, she was ahead of me and may or may not have seen the tree door jutting out from where she stood). From where I was positioned, I could see that the tree door was definitely open. And the "vision" I'd had in my trance was of the door shut—was this true, or just another false memory?

I argued: "It makes no sense that I would manufacture a memory like that. What's the point of it? In my mind's eye, I clearly saw the door shut."

Helen pursed her lips as if pursuing this thought, but my impression is that she thought I had gone off the proverbial deep end. Visions, delusions—same difference! This was not objective proof. I couldn't stand in a court of law and defend any of this.

Helen asked the cop outside to come inside and get inside the tree. Once inside the tree, he was asked to lock the tree door from the inside. We stayed where we were.

Once the door was locked, it was again unmistakable. The door was closed, and we could see that. The contour was smooth.

It was clear (to me, at least) that I had really seen what I remembered seeing.

But Helen remained unconvinced.

"With all due respect," she began and snorted one of her impressive snorts, "this is nuts. What you're saying is that you remember that the door was closed when we opened the door and came inside. What you're also saying is that while all of us, detectives, cops, and pathologists, were inside the room, somebody opened the inside tree door and came inside the room. The major flaw in your argument is that *we didn't see this person.* The least we can expect when a person suddenly pops into a room is that we *see* that person. Since we didn't see any such person materializing in the room, it follows that no such person actually came into the room. Also, why would this person do a silly thing like that? Why come into a room full of cops? Why? Because you want to get caught? No-no-no-no-no."

I have to admit I didn't have an answer for her. All her points were valid.

I didn't want to give up, though. Something told me I was right, that I really did remember what I remembered, and that what I remembered was an actual fact, the truth. I didn't think it was a fake memory.

I stepped inside the tree. It was a bit musty inside. I pulled the door shut.

It was then that I noticed a shaft of bright light coming through something like a peephole. In fact, this was not "something like a peephole"…it *was* a peephole. I put my eye on this peephole.

It was a larger peephole than the ones I am familiar with. It was about the width of three fingers—I mean my fingers, which are on the average side. It was about as wide as my eye. When I looked through it, I had a panoramic view of a large area of the study. I could see what was to the left, who was to the right, and who was right up ahead.

So, theoretically, it was possible for someone to be inside the tree and get a good glimpse of who, or what, was around. Such a person could easily enter the room while the room was full of people and not be seen immediately—but only because the tree was sort of tucked away in the back corner of the room, by the bookshelves. All this person would have to make sure was that somebody was not actually standing close to the tree at the time of coming out of it—and this was possible to do so with such an enormous peephole, with the special kind of lens it had in it. But naturally, once he came out, he couldn't stand there for too long or move out of the room without being noticed. I mean, there was no way. If he really came out that way, he would have to be seen, if not immediately, then a few minutes later at the most.

I explained my point of view to Helen. She peeked through it just as I had and made an unfunny, vulgar remark about peep shows. She held her ground.

"OK, I'll grant you that he's able to come out when people are not around the tree, and it's in the back of the room, I agree. Even if he comes out like you say he did, what did he do after that? He couldn't just have stood there! He had to leave the room, right? And even if he stayed where he was, we'd eventually see him. There were cops all over the room, Imogene, everywhere! I didn't see somebody just standing there by the tree, holding a head and a weapon. You didn't see any such person, did you?"

There was no denying that. I mumbled something like, "But I was studying the corpse, and I was preoccupied. You know what I said about the gorilla—I was distracted by all the other drama in the room."

"This gorilla…" I bet Helen considered using strong language to put down my gorilla concept but changed her mind. "All right, let us say he did enter the room because no one was around, and I admit to you that that is possible. Let me repeat: *Then what?* Did he just vanish into thin air after that? Because, gorilla or no gorilla, I don't remember seeing anybody who wasn't supposed to be there. Maybe he was disguised as a gorilla. That would certainly explain why no one saw him!"

63

"Dr. Chaplin claims that you looked surprised when you entered the room. Can you tell me anything about it?"

Perkins answered without expression: "I had seen my employer decapitated. Surely, most people would call that surprising."

"Possible. But is there anything else—something that you are not telling us?"

"I cannot imagine what you may be referring to."

"I can. What if you knew how this murder was committed? What if Mr. Zimaresh had told you or asked you to help him in some way? After all, he was your employer, and I've always heard that you valets will do anything your masters tell you to."

Helen was doing her best to be maximally obnoxious. But, in my opinion, Perkins was not the kind of man on whom such tricks worked. These valets or butlers are made of some impervious substance, like steel, and nothing moves them. Perkins was not about to begin cooperating simply because Helen was being tough.

He answered impassively,

"Another thing you may have heard about gentlemen's gentlemen—or valets—is that they are exceedingly loyal to their masters. If my master had indeed confided in me and solicited my help, what makes you imagine that I would tell you, of all people?"

I looked at him. He had said these words in a very matter-of-fact way. He was seated comfortably before us. Comfortable but alert, in an attentive manner, deferential and subservient, it seemed to me. But at the same time, he was not scared of Helen and her bulldog methods. He caught me looking at him and nodded.

"If you know something," Helen growled, "It would be best to tell us. How does prison sound to you?"

"Unappealing, madam. But if I may be permitted to inquire, on what grounds would I be imprisoned?"

"Obstruction of justice. Not telling us what you know."

"But I know so little. The master was an ingenious man, fond of creating the most incredible illusions and puzzles. He was always playing tricks and riddles, daring me to solve them."

"So this is just another riddle?"

"It *is* a riddle. A diabolical riddle, I will admit. My only knowledge of the crime business comes from the works of Mr. Zimaresh, but I think it would be fair to say that before you throw someone in prison, you require something along the lines of proof. Is that a correct assumption? From the way it appears to an outsider like me, you are no closer to determining how the murder was committed. It follows that if you are unaware of how it was done, you cannot formulate a reasonable hypothesis of who did it because how did whoever did it manage to do it? Wouldn't judge and jury require some evidence, something about the mechanics of the business? Or is it that, like savages in uncivilized countries, you believe in torturing confessions out of people? Is it your intention to incarcerate me and pull out my nails or apply electrodes to my unmentionables?"

Helen had turned a shade of some color between red and purple. Her nostrils were flaring. Given the slightest opportunity, I could easily see her storming into a torture chamber, applying electrodes to Perkins's "unmentionables," just for the fun of it. Not that she would really do it, but I could picture her enjoying it tremendously.

"This is not a joke. It is a very serious matter," Helen said, sounding a bit like a peevish schoolteacher.

"It is serious business, madam," Perkins said gravely. "And therefore, I believe you should make a serious attempt at solving it instead of badgering people who know nothing about it. I understand you must do what you are doing, but I have to set the record straight. I am afraid I can be of no help."

"Perkins," I said. I felt I had to break in, not because I hoped to get anywhere, but because I had to. The atmosphere was turning very hostile. "Perkins, I know you saw something. Something caught your eye. Let me remind you. You had just entered the room, and you saw something. What was it? Please, Perkins, if you can tell us, it would be a great help…" I ended pleadingly, hoping to appeal to the man in him.

Perkins answered softly. "Madam, I don't know what I can tell you…"

Abruptly, Helen changed the subject: "Did somebody come to visit Mr. Zimaresh on the day of his murder?"

"Yes, madam, he had a party. Many people were here. His friends, his family, his publishers, his publicist, his filmmaker—scores of people."

"No, I mean before the party?"

Perkins was silent. He then looked at me. I maintained an eager, pleading look.

"Mr. Marion Best and his associate," he said quietly.

"The associate was a large man?"

"Exceedingly tall and very large."

"When?"

"Three or so hours before the party."

"What did they do? How long did they stay there?"

"I don't know. Mr. Zimaresh asked me to retire to my quarters. He indicated he didn't need me."

"Did you go to your room?"

"Naturally. He had clearly told me that he didn't want me around."

"So you can't tell me when Best and his friend left?"

"No, I cannot. I did not see them leave."

"Where did Mr. Zimaresh take them?"

"To his study."

Nobody spoke for a few minutes.

"Are you sure there's nothing more you can tell us—about what Dr. Chaplin thinks you may have seen?" Even Helen was taking the gentle approach. It was clearly more effective.

"Alas," he shook his head, "Will you excuse me, please? I think I hear the doorbell."

"I didn't hear anything," said Helen.

"Madam is not a valet. I am trained to hear doorbells. Ours is malfunctioning and is a trifle soft. May I be excused momentarily?"

"Go ahead," said Helen wearily.

64

It took us a little while to realize that he had given us what is referred to as "the slip." In other words, after telling us that he had gone to answer the doorbell, he actually gathered up his essential belongings (they must have been already packed) and left by the front door. He was seen by a neighbor who told us that he walked out. Did he seem to be in a hurry? No. He walked out at a leisurely pace as if he was going for a stroll around the block. Yes, he was carrying something. A briefcase. Where did he turn to? This, the neighbor didn't know. After all, he was just the butler or something, and a butler is really below the radar screen when you're a big-shot CEO of a prominent company in Houston (which is what the neighbor turned out to be, even though he looked rather un-prominent in an unflattering pair of pale pink pajamas).

As you may imagine, the effect of this discovery on Helen Freud was profound. She reminded me of those cartoon characters who have been made jackasses of, and they suddenly work out that they've been suckered. Like Bugs Bunny or some such wily character, Perkins, with great aplomb and presence of mind, had made his escape. Why? We would soon find out.

His room was neat. Not a thing out of place. His closet appeared undisturbed, full of the kinds of clothes a gentleman's gentleman, a valet, is supposed to wear. Black suits, crisp white shirts. In one corner was lighter wear: T-shirts, corduroy pants, jeans: this is what Perkins wore on the days he wasn't supposed to be prim and proper Perkins. There was a box of tools: screwdrivers, an Allen wrench—almost everything you'd need around the house for fix-ups.

Helen was pouting like a sour prune, her face an unpleasant mix of disappointment and anger.

"What's this?" she said, pouncing on a piece of paper, neatly folded, with the words: "PLEASE READ THIS."

She unfolded this paper with the speed of an adolescent trying to get into another adolescent's pants. She fumbled. The paper had been folded into sixteenths, which is the name one could give to what you get when you fold it first into four quadrants and then again into four. I suppose there is a mathematical formula that governs this sort of folding, but this is neither the time nor the place to go into the mathematics of paper folding. Suffice it to say that the paper, a neatly folded one, showed the elegant handwriting of Perkins.

This is what he had written:

I have to leave. My life is in danger. I need a critical piece of the proof. I will explain all.

But first, I have to prove that I wasn't a part of any of this. I truly wasn't. I swear to it. I give you my word that I had nothing to do with this. If she finds out, I will be dead before too long. I will not name any names yet. You will hear from me soon once I have acquired the essential proof. Yours sincerely, Perkins.

Helen read this out in a flat, unemotional voice, totally devoid of the drama, the sense of danger that the letter immediately conveyed. After she had finished reading it, she read it a second time, more slowly, similarly without emotion. Finally, she repeated only the following sentence from the letter:

"If she finds out, I will be dead before too long."

"Who's she?" I asked, echoing her thoughts.

"Yes. Who's she?"

We actually had a long list of "she's." There were his mistresses, his wives, and anyone from his circle who stood to gain from his death. I suppose his publicist, his business partners, and other males who benefited from his demise were excluded on the grounds that they were most definitely not *she*-s. Unless Perkins was lying, but the letter sounded so sincere. That said, liars can sound sincere, so sincere—just look around, and you'll see a whole bunch of sincere politicians, the majority of whom are liars, as we all know. But what if Perkins was not lying? Then we had a dangerous *she*, a *she* who had precipitated the deaths of three individuals: Zimaresh, Felicity Moon, and Spriggs.

"Amelia Zimaresh," I said with great confidence. It made sense. Who else? Amelia stood to gain the most from her father's death. If he had engineered the whole affair (and it was obvious that he had), who else to trust but his own flesh and blood, an ambitious, greedy daughter? He was going to die anyway. Amelia could've easily agreed to work with Marion Best and his less-than-bright giant of an associate, a man who could've been especially handy with a sword or an axe. We knew that Best and Mark had been there on the day of the murder. So they could've done the deed and then somehow managed to vanish from the scene of the crime. Amelia wouldn't even have needed to be in the room with them. Surely, it must be an exceedingly unpleasant task to decapitate your own father, no matter how willing he was or how greedy you were. Once the crime was planned, she could be at the party and maintain a cast-iron alibi.

This is the gist of what I told Helen. Helen, thoughtful, said, "Possible. But I have another candidate for a 'she.'"

"Who?" I asked—though a moment's reflection should have brought me to the same conclusion as Helen.

65

The other "she" was Marion Best's wife, Ingrid.

"She's an actress too. Not a great one, and not an employed one, which means she's as poor as a church mouse. But an actress can act, and she could've been putting on an act," Helen said. "Point number two: she finds the head. How convenient is that? Nobody is going to think that she would be part of a crime like this and then find the head in her own house. She could've simply tied a brick to it and tossed the head in a lake! Her finding the head, some defense attorney will say, proves that she is innocent. You don't kill someone, and then you keep the evidence around—how stupid is that? Finding the head is a great way of keeping suspicion away from her. Point number three: Assuming that Best has left town, does it make sense that that big child could go around murdering people—I mean Spriggs—all on his own, without getting anything wrong or getting caught in the process? No. Murder's not easy, especially not a complicated one like this. He had to have guidance. Support. And who's the best person to guide him? A total stranger? Unlikely. Perkins? Possible, I suppose, but why—and how likely is it that Mark would take direction from Perkins? Marion Best? He's not in town, though he could be hiding—guiding Mark—but that big lug wouldn't be able to keep it secret. Amelia Zimaresh? I don't think so. She would want to keep as far as possible from him. What if he blurted out the truth, 'Miss Amelia said this-or-that, or Miss Amelia told me to do so-and-so.' No. The less information he has, the better."

"But," I argued. "The same could be said of Mrs. Best. He could tell on her as well, without meaning to. What's to stop him from babbling that 'Mrs. Best told me to do that?'"

"Good point. So maybe Marion Best is the person who's doing all the dirty work. My guess is that all Mark was needed for was manpower. To swing the axe or sword, etc. Once that was done, his part was done. Then, all he could tell us is that Marion Best was there when he swung the axe. We'd try to find Marion, but he is nowhere. He's probably in South America or somewhere. For all we know, Mrs. Best intends to join him soon. As far as Mark knows, Mrs. Best has nothing to do with any of this. She's the poor lamb who found the horrible head of Mr. Zimaresh."

Mrs. Best could certainly be the *she* in question. But why would a man like Perkins be so afraid of such a petite little *she*? Something was missing from the equation. What?

66

Helen Freud called Ingrid Best and Mark in for questioning. It was pretty late, close to midnight. I am summarizing the interview that took place (Helen Freud gave me the transcript, from which I've extracted the essence for you).

Naturally, they were offered an attorney, but Mrs. Best declined, saying she had nothing to hide—or tell. Her story was simple and unhelpful. How could she know how the head had ended up outside her backdoor? Was she some kind of idiotic freak who would decapitate someone, stick the head—a human head—behind her house, pretend to discover it, go into shock, and then call the police? According to her, anybody who suggested such an absurd sequence of events was in need of considerable psychological help.

She didn't—or wouldn't—believe that Marion was capable of hurting anyone. The whole story was nonsense. She couldn't say where Marion was. He had told her he was going to L.A. for a possible job. A role in a good film. He didn't want to tell her more so as not to get her hopes high or jinx his chances. She had no idea that instead of going to L.A., he had gone to Zimaresh's house with Mark.

She and Marion were Mark's neighbors and the closest thing he had to guardians. He had no family or siblings; he did have a caretaker in the house, an old woman named Doris, who was fairly crazy herself. When Mark's grandmother died (the only relative Mark had for the longest time), she left a small inheritance to Mark. And Doris. Doris was a friend of Mark's late grandmother. She was such a good friend, in fact, that she agreed to be a mother, grandmother, and guardian to Mark. She must have done a good job because Mark had stayed out of harm's way for so many years. Until now, it seemed.

Marion Best and his wife had moved into the house next to Mark's five years ago, got chummy with Mark and Doris, and became like family. Doris was there, at the police station, as a matter of fact. Naturally, she had insisted on coming along. She sat glumly in the room during the questioning.

But all Mark could tell Freud was this: Yes, he had gone to Mr. Zimaresh's house with Marion Best yesterday. Mr. Zimaresh had been very kind. He'd offered him a muffin, some cookies, even an ice cream. Then Mr. Zimaresh and Marion had gone away. Finally, somebody had come back with a message from Marion—a message to look after his wife. A message Mark promptly crumpled up and dropped in the trash can after he was helped to read it.

Who helped him read it?

Why, the person who brought him the message, of course.

And who was that?

Mark couldn't say who it was. It wasn't Zimaresh. It was a woman. Her hair was in a bun, and she wore dark glasses. Nobody he knew. Mark was unable to provide a better description.

So, here was another *she*. Freud had no reason to believe that Mark was lying. He wasn't intelligent enough to create a lie of this magnitude.

I now come to the most surprising part of his story. He told her he cut his foot on a sharp rock while waiting outside Zimaresh's house for the cab to take him home. Herein lies a tale: Very simply, the woman asked him to give his shoes to her. Mark didn't want to, but she told him that Marion really, really wanted the shoes. If Marion wanted them, Mark couldn't say no, could he? So it was natural for Mark to hand them over, and Mark ended up without any shoes, barefoot (he wasn't wearing socks), and that was how he cut his foot.

Where were those shoes?

In answer, Mark pointed to his shoes. He was wearing them! How did he get those shoes back? Helen asked him. Mark answered her simply,

"They were there the next day, on the doorstep, when I came back."
Came back from where? "From the woods, of course, right behind my
house," he answered. "What were you doing in the woods?" Helen inquired. "I was taking a walk," he told her.

Why would somebody want his shoes? The reason could only be as
follows: Assuming Mark wasn't lying—a reasonable assumption—
Zimaresh, the mystery writer, was staging a clue. He needed his shoes to
create the bloody footprints. The footprints from large feet. Except in this
case, the foot inside the shoes belonged to someone else. A she, or a he,
who didn't really have large feet.

Freud showed Mark a picture of Amelia Zimaresh. His face was blank.
He didn't recognize her.

PART THREE: ANOTHER BODY

67

It was close to four in the morning when the call came. The phone must have rung several times before I woke up because Helen Freud was grumpy and complained that I had no business sleeping so soundly when so much was happening. "What's happened?" I asked her, barely able to mouth the words. "Perkins happened," she told me. What she meant was not that Perkins had happened—whatever that is supposed to mean—but that, very likely, he was dead. I say very likely because of the following:

Briefly, somebody had called Freud. A woman, trying to disguise her voice by whispering and speaking hoarsely. She told Helen that Perkins was where he deserved to be, in the woods behind the Best residence. Helen tried to ask her what Perkins was doing in those woods in the middle of the night, but the woman hung up. The implication was clear. Perkins had passed on.

So there I was again, at yet another scene, my fourth murder scene in two days. Simon, the investigator, was there with me as usual (he picked me up), and he and I, in about an hour, found ourselves in the thick of the woods. These were dense woods behind the homes of Best and Mark, the very woods, in fact, where Mark took his walks. Now, any sane person would never take a walk here, but Mark was not, strictly speaking, sane. But he had little to fear. He was a large, frightful-looking man, much more likely to scare off anyone with bad intentions.

The woods closed around you like an embrace, an unpleasant embrace, an embrace you could do without. However, as you went deep into it (we did), they cleared out a bit. There were patches here and there that were spread out and less densely wooded, but you had to wade through the dense portions to get to them. Our goal, helped by the dogs, was to get to where the anonymous female caller had said Perkins would be found. Obviously, Perkins was not just sitting there with an umbrella (it had rained on and off), reading a book by flashlight, waiting for us. As I've said already, all things pointed to Perkins being dead.

And finally, we were there. A sparsely wooded area suddenly opened up before us, giving us a nasty, though expected, revelation.

A body. Not just a body, which was bad enough, but a body that had been savagely hacked with an axe. The axe in question had been thrown a few yards away from the body.

Simon and I sifted through the evidence. First, the blood. It had soaked into the ground, which had turned a burgundy red. Next, the head: it had rolled off to a side. It was badly chopped up, unrecognizable, almost as if the killer had spared no effort in *making it* unrecognizable. In fact, it took a moment to figure out that it was the head. The hands were partially cut off—evidently, the murderer had tried to cut them off and then changed his or her mind. The feet were similarly incompletely severed. There were deep gashes above the knees, but the murderer had not succeeded in amputating the legs. The murderer had sliced into the skin with the axe, apparently randomly. Instead of cutting through the body, he had attacked the surface of the skin in order to disfigure it.

The end result was that there was virtually no skin over large chunks of the lower legs, the knees, the thighs, arms, and portions of the trunk.

I felt the familiar, unpleasant feeling of nausea. I scrunched up my nose, and the feeling passed. The murderer had put the axe to such ghastly use that I doubted that, short of DNA analysis, we would ever know for sure whose body it was.

Perkins was the logical candidate. Next to the axe was a briefcase. We opened it. There were a pair of folded shirts, plain white, a couple of pants, one blue, one black, and a plane ticket to London, made out for Perkins.

Also, a passport belonging to Perkins. Finally, in an envelope was a small note:

For the police
The money was the price for his silence. His life is the price for not shutting up.

There was no money in the briefcase. If Perkins had brought any cash with him, the murderer had removed it. Unless, of course, Perkins was the murderer himself, but why would he leave his passport and tickets behind?

"Pretty bad, huh?" Helen said.

"Too brutal. I mean, why try to chop everything off? Isn't it enough that he's cut off the man's head? He still wanted to try to hack off the hands, feet, and knees, make a mess of the skin…"

"Can you prove this is Perkins?"

"Unless we can find Perkins's doctor to supply us with a DNA sample to which we can compare the DNA from the body…I don't think it's possible from here," I ventured. "The killer's made short work of the head. He's really mucked it up. I suppose we could try to X-ray his teeth and find Perkins's dentist to give us a dental X-ray on him, but I can't imagine his teeth are okay after the brute went at them with his axe."

"So you're saying…"

"I don't know," I said. The basic forensic teaching is that if somebody disfigures the body or identifying features on the body, it is to conceal the identity of the victim.

"It could be Perkins. If the killer was really upset with him…" I said.

Freud snorted. "Upset! Now that's an understatement!"

"Perkins or not?" I wondered aloud. "The murderer has left Perkins's stuff here, hoping that we will think that the victim is Perkins—in which case the murderer is Perkins, and this is somebody else—but who? Anyway, possibility number two is this: the victim is Perkins, and the murderer, the *she*-murderer, was so furious that she made short work of him with an axe. Which is it? I don't think we can decide without evidence—DNA evidence, dental evidence, whatever we can lay our hands on."

I stumbled on a rock, nearly falling, but I was caught by one of the cops there.

"Thanks, Tom," I said.

"Not Tom," he said. "I'm Gus. Tom's the guy over there."

I saw Tom. I'd spoken to him shortly after arriving on the scene. Really, Tom was nothing like Gus. The two looked about as similar as Madonna and Mother Teresa.

Hopeless, I thought. What marvelous observation skills! About perfect for a situation like this.

And then, without any warning, it all came together. I had a sudden moment of *ah-ha*. You know what I mean? *Ah-ha*—a realization. You see, I was looking at the final piece of the puzzle, the one that put it all together for me. My brain was working out the details behind the scenes, subconsciously, and needed this last bit of information to reach a conclusion. I am not an expert on what my brain does or doesn't do subconsciously. All I know is that I had figured it all out. I clearly saw what Perkins had seen when he had entered the study. Like him, I now saw the gorilla. I knew what I had missed—and why.

PART FOUR: SEEING THE GORILLA

68

It was quite simple. The way it had unfolded had made it confusing.

But the veil was lifted. The final clue was a combo clue of Tom the cop, Gus the cop, and the chopped-up fourth body. Specifically, the fact that the killer had tried to axe off the hands, the feet, and most importantly, the knees. And the fact that he—it was a *he* and not a *she*—had cut into the skin to disfigure it. This final clue brought home all the other clues to me. Particularly the clue of what Perkins might have seen in that room that day—the all-important vision, the one that I had missed until now.

I hope I am not needlessly mystifying—it is not my intention to do so. I am accurately trying to tell, in as clear a fashion as possible, how the truth suddenly clicked into place inside my head. It sounds confusing, and so I will break up the truth and present it systematically.

First, what we knew, or thought we knew:

Zimaresh had created a mystery for us, a real-life mystery, one that involved his own death, to give his dwindled fortune a boost, to leave behind an increased legacy to his daughter and others. He created an impossible murder, full of blood, camel blood, which he obtained by becoming a board member of a new zoo in Houston. He created the mystery of the big-footed accomplice but, in reality, had merely borrowed Mark's shoes to create this incorrect impression. Initially, I had imagined that Zimaresh was still alive, that he was, therefore, a ruthless killer, and that somebody else sat dead and headless in his place, but then, Zimaresh's head was found, and so it was hardly possible that he was still alive or the murderer. We had established that Felicity Moon's murder was committed by Spriggs, an employee of the medical examiner's office, who was supplying information to Zimaresh and his accomplice (or accomplices) about me, the most inexperienced idiot around, the perfect fool to botch up the case. No doubt the unfortunate Dr. Moon had seen Spriggs put the letter from Zimaresh on my desk. Spriggs came up from behind, knocked her out, and then drove a knife into her, a knife he had borrowed from the morgue. He made the error of leaving the stuff in the men's room, casting doubt on his story that a woman was behind this crime. Later, we found Spriggs dead. He knew too much and was too much of a liability. He had to be taken care of in the most final way possible. Who had killed Spriggs? At first, I believed it was Zimaresh, but then Zimaresh's head turned up. So it had to be someone else. Right?

Right.

Or, perhaps wrong.

But how could it be wrong? How can a murdered, headless man commit a murder? If Zimaresh were murdered—and he had to be—we had his head—then how could he commit somebody else's murder?

The answer: What if a murdered, headless man is not really murdered or headless? No, I don't mean that Zimaresh wasn't dead. No. The head we had found was definitely his, and so he was, without a doubt, dead. But even so—

I see that I am doing it again. Looking over these words, it might appear that I'm not making much sense. Instead of making things clear, I'm confusing them. But bear with me, and all will become clear.

And, as I said, it was all because I saw the hacked-up corpse with a disfigured, smashed, unrecognizable head, partially chopped knees, and gashes in the skin. And Tom and Gus.

This is what I told Helen,

"This can't be Perkins! In fact, it is not Perkins. I'm certain of it!"

"Not Perkins?"

"Of course. You can't identify this corpse. Listen, if this were Perkins, why would the killer smash the body in such a way that we wouldn't be able to tell that this was Perkins? He wouldn't have needed to leave the suitcase behind, with a note, trying to make us think that this is Perkins. This is a forced, very crude attempt to make us believe that we have Perkins's body here. But this is not Perkins. And if this is not Perkins, merely someone trying to make us think it is Perkins, and Perkins is not to be found anywhere, then it follows Perkins is responsible for this crime."

"If not Perkins, who is it then?"

This was the insight that I had. My one genuine Sherlock Holmes or Hercule Poirot moment. One that I am quite proud of, I must add.

"I think the head belongs to Marion Best and the rest of the body to George Zimaresh."

Helen's response was a silence, followed by a breathless, "What?"

"I will explain. Listen. At first, we found the headless body, right? There was no way to identify it. Two witnesses, Zimaresh's daughter and his ex-lover, Magdalene Fitzpatrick, *told us that Zimaresh had a large mole on his knee.* In fact, his ex-mistress had visited Zimaresh a few hours before the party to lend him a CD and had not noticed the mole was missing— Zimaresh was wearing shorts. Maybe, if it hadn't been there, she might have noted this. Second, Amelia Z. was insistent that her father didn't want the mole removed. So, let us assume that the mole was not removed. There was no scar on the knee or any evidence of a recent surgical procedure at the knee. If we say Zimaresh still had his mole, then we immediately note, *importantly, that our first corpse-minus-head, let's call it corpse A, had no such mole on the knee.* Now we have *another corpse, corpse B,* but we can't tell whether the knee had a mole or not. Because the killer tried to cut the knees off, and failing that, tried to cut into them as badly or as *effectively* as he could to make sure *that we'd never be able to tell if one of the knees had a huge mole or not—not a shard of visible skin remains.* Now, the head. It's smashed. There is no way to tell whose it is. *That's perfect because the killer wants to hide the fact that it's not Perkins's head.* The body is that of Zimaresh, I am convinced, and the head can't be Zimaresh's because Zimaresh's head is sitting in a cooler in the morgue. So whose body is in the morgue, the first headless body? I think the smashed head *here* and the *first* corpse in the morgue go together. And I think they both belong to Marion Best."

"The body in Zimaresh's study was Marion Best's, and the head—this head, the smashed head here is Marion Best's. Is that what you're saying?"

"Yes. It all fits," I said. I pieced it together. "Zimaresh paid Marion Best some money—that producer, Ray Marsh—told us that. I think what happened next is that Best then told his wife that he was going to Los Angeles. In reality, he went with Mark to Zimaresh's house. Mark was simply there to provide a bunch of useless clues. While Mark waits, Marion goes inside. Maybe he's drugged or something or in a suitable state of compliance, ready to be decapitated. Now Mark tells us that someone, a woman, came to give him a note from Marion, the note asking Mark to take care of Mrs. Best, and this woman took his shoes as well. The woman was, I believe, either Perkins or Zimaresh disguised as a woman. So now Perkins and Zimaresh behead Marion before the party, spill camel blood everywhere, create a new set of footprints with Mark's shoes and move the body into Zimaresh's study. Perkins then goes somewhere with the head and the weapon, leaving Zimaresh behind. He returns. The party begins. Zimaresh is in the study. His room is soundproof, but it has a public announcement system. He turns it on, shouts that he's being decapitated, screams, and then all of us, you, me, everybody, end up in the room after breaking open the door that could only be locked from the inside. And it was locked—by Zimaresh."

I stopped to take a breath. I was giddy, breathless with excitement. It was the rush of suddenly knowing after frustratingly not knowing for so long.

"All right. Let's say you're right," Helen said, "It explains why we don't have a head or a weapon in the room. But there's still Zimaresh.

According to you, he was still inside the room when we entered. Why didn't we see him?"

I was prepared for that. In fact, that's what I realized when I bumped into the cop "Tom"—who was actually another uniformed cop, Gus. At that instant, I saw what Perkins must have seen when he entered the room. The thing that caught his eye, the thing that made him stop surprised, so surprised that he lost his poise and became, for a moment, disoriented.

"It's because we were looking for a man with a weapon, an axe, maybe this very axe that is here on the ground, and a head in a bag. But the weapon and head were no longer there, as we've agreed. Only one person in the room remained. Zimaresh. How does he get out? Well, I think he may have hidden inside the tree. Through the big peephole, he can see all of us in the room. You, me, cops everywhere. At the appropriate moment, when he sees that he can come out without being noticed, he takes a chance and comes out, and then he leaves the room. And nobody sees him!"

"Brilliant. One question, though. Why does no one see him?"

"Easy," I said. "It's like the invisible gorilla. *People were not expecting to see a gorilla, so they didn't see it.* Zimaresh pulled a gorilla out of his hat for this trick. It's almost childish. I didn't see it till right now. Remember me telling you that Perkins had seen something? For the life of me, I couldn't figure out what he'd seen. Not until a few minutes ago. But let me prove it to you. Perkins helps Zimaresh commit the murder. Why? Because he has faith in his master. He knows the master has figured out a way to get out of the room. It's one of his puzzles. Perkins had told us that Zimaresh liked creating these puzzles—he liked playing these games with him and others. Remember what he told us: *He was always playing tricks and riddles, daring me to solve them.* So, I believe that Perkins *didn't know **how*** Zimaresh was going to get out of the room. But he had faith that Zimaresh had worked out a practically foolproof method of escaping from under our very noses. He could still get caught, but as we know, he didn't."

Helen clicked her tongue with exasperation. "You're driving me crazy. How the hell did he get out?"

"*I think he was disguised as a cop in uniform, like the othere uniformed cops in there.* When I just mixed Tom and Gus up—it put me on the right track. Nobody was paying attention to cops leaving and entering the scene. It was absolute chaos there—it shouldn't have been. But for all we knew, a dangerous killer was in the room with a sharp weapon. We needed all the cops we could get. And Zimaresh had made sure that there was a huge number of uniformed cops there. He, Perkins, some guests had made 911 calls. And Zimaresh himself made calls to individual cops from the private phone in his study as well. So all these cops were looking for a killer with an axe or a sword and a human head. *No cop was looking for another cop.* A cop can come and go as he pleases without anyone paying attention to him. This is what Perkins realized. He had made one 911 call himself because he had been ordered to by Zimaresh, and it had probably puzzled him: *Why is the boss so apparently crazy? Why is he begging to be caught?* Once he entered the room and saw all those cops, he immediately realized. The boss was dressed up as a cop and had left the scene. *This is why the inside tree door was open! Because Zimaresh had entered the room from the tree when he saw through the peephole that there was a good chance to do so.* I know you thought it was silly of me to go into the hypnotic trance or whatever, but I am sure that when I entered the room, the inside tree door was closed, just as I remembered when I was in that trance. Obviously, the only time when both the inside and outside tree doors could be closed was when there was somebody inside the tunnel between them since the tree doors could only be locked from the inside. *Even if I imagined the closed tree door, the only way that he could have been hidden momentarily was inside that trunk. It was the only temporary hiding spot inside the room.* Anyway, Zimaresh came out. He was dressed as a cop, so nobody saw him, he left the scene and he disappeared."

"But why take such a chance? He could still get caught."

"I think the chance was worth it. Even if he got caught, his books would still sell like mad. Can you imagine the headlines? *Dying mystery author decapitates victim!* People are crazy. When someone's in the news in a sensational way, you can't help going to the bookstore to buy everything he's written. There's no such thing as bad publicity. Either way, whether he gets caught or not, his books and that of his daughter are guaranteed to sell."

"But why did Perkins go along with it? If we caught Zimaresh, he could have told everything!"

"I think that Zimaresh and Perkins must have had an understanding of some kind. If Zimaresh got caught leaving the room, Perkins could leave very quickly. Nobody needed to know about his involvement till it was too late."

Helen closed her eyes.

"Can you prove all this?"

"I think I can and very easily. We can match the DNA from this corpse, corpse B here, with the DNA from Zimaresh's head and prove they're the same, and we can match the DNA from the smashed head here with the first headless corpse. Maybe Marion has a DNA sample sitting somewhere. If he does, we can compare that to the first corpse and to the head here. And, of course, you could just catch Perkins and make him talk."

69

To make a long story short:

They did catch Perkins. He was disguised as a woman, but a very unconvincing one with thin, prickly hairs on the upper lip. Perkins had gotten careless as a woman; maybe he was too eager to escape and had let slip a few details. He was trying to catch a plane to Spain as "Mrs. Ernestina Perkins"—his mother. Mrs. Perkins had died some years ago, but her passport was still valid. Perkins looked like his mother, but something about him, maybe his nervousness, attracted the airport official's attention. That, and the fact that the wig fell off when he dropped his passport and bent down to pick it up. That really gave him away.

Once he was caught, he made no attempt to conceal facts. Perkins is a practical man and knows when it is futile to try and escape. You won't catch Perkins doing crazy heroics (I am writing in the present tense because he is here, in Houston, in prison, for the remainder of his life). He confirmed what I had suspected. He helped Zimaresh kill Marion. In addition to his loyalty to his employer, Zimaresh had slipped in half a million dollars to sweeten the deal. After Marion was killed, Perkins went off to the woods behind Best's house and temporarily hid Marion's head in a hole. Zimaresh escaped, as I have described. Perkins didn't know how Zimaresh was going to do it, but once he entered the room, he understood almost immediately. He was so surprised at the audacity of it that he was momentarily stunned. Perkins and Zimaresh did have an agreement: Perkins would leave if Zimaresh got caught. Perkins had the passport on him, and he could turn into his dead mother (ineffectively, as we have seen) at a moment's notice.

Zimaresh's informant in our office was Spriggs. He committed the murder of Felicity Moon, as I've already explained, when she caught him putting the letter on my desk. Later on, Zimaresh strangled him—but we have Perkins's word on this, and he could be lying, but I don't think so. Whatever. Later on, Perkins killed Zimaresh, as per plan, in the woods behind Best's house after Zimaresh was suitably drugged. These woods were (and remain) sufficiently dense yet deserted and scary-looking to prevent being frequented by others. It was then that Perkins chopped up Zimaresh's body with the axe, doing his best to conceal the mole on the left knee. He couldn't just disfigure the left knee—that would be too obvious—so he tried to do as good a hatchet job as he could on the *entire* body. It took effort and sweat, but he got it done eventually. He tried to hack off the knees, but that proved to be too difficult, so he sliced into the knees as savagely as he could till he was satisfied that no one could see the mole on Zimaresh's knee. He then chopped up Marion's head as best as he could to make it completely unrecognizable.

Then, Perkins packed the head, that is to say, Zimaresh's head, in a bucket filled with ice, walked over to Best's house, left it behind the backdoor, and threw some pebbles at the window to alert her. She came out, saw it, fainted, and the rest you know.

Why did he finally decide to run away?

"The situation was getting decidedly uncomfortable. I was not sure how long I could carry on this deception."

Oh, and before I forget, there was supposed to be a fifth victim. Yours truly. I mean me. Perkins was to deliver me a knife in the chest and leave a completed manuscript at the scene, detailing Zimaresh's method. The manuscript was hand-written by Zimaresh himself and not very long. About ten pages or so. He had composed it shortly before the first murder. It was hand-written so that nobody could have any doubts about who had written it (it was conclusively determined by handwriting experts to have been written by Zimaresh himself).

In this brief document, Zimaresh basically went over his thinking process, how he planned it, how far back it went (shortly after he was diagnosed with terminal cancer), his bureaucratic encounters with the board of the new Metropolitan Zoo, the fact that he and Perkins had stolen into the zoo in the early hours of the morning and wounded the baby camel's foot, creating a need for the camel blood. Then Zimaresh himself stole the blood and stored it in the fridge in his house, right next to the milk.

Perkins claims he had no intentions of killing me. He had, in fact, dropped the manuscript in the mail addressed to Helen Freud. "I like Dr. Chaplin. It wouldn't have been proper to do away with her," he told Helen.

Well, thank heavens for that.

It's a pity that Marion had to die. But then, somebody usually has to so that somebody else can make a great deal of money. And money was made, quite a bit of it, by the Zimaresh estate and by his daughter Amelia in particular.

And finally, let me pay tribute to modern science, without which all this would be conjecture. Despite all efforts to viciously destroy the bodies and body parts, DNA matches were made successfully. Zimaresh's head and the last mutilated body had identical DNA, just as the first body and the smashed head at the last crime scene shared identical DNA. We could never conclusively prove that they belonged to Marion, however, because Marion, ironically, was a surprisingly healthy individual and never so much as visited a dentist or a doctor.

We had to take Zimaresh's hand-written manuscript and Perkins's word for it.